Showdown

Montana Bred Series
Book 3

LINDA BRADLEY

Akin House Publishing

SHOWDOWN
Copyright ©2024
Print Edition
LINDA BRADLEY

Cover Design by: Nancie Rowe Janitz Designs

Published in the United States of America by AKIN HOUSE PUBLISHING.

ISBN: 978-0-9995793-9-8

DEDICATION

For Grace

"Apparently, everyone is the catalyst
of their own story."
–Chloe McIntyre

ACKNOWLEDGMENTS

Thank you, dear readers! I have thoroughly enjoyed writing Chloe McIntyre's story. Montana captivated my attention some years ago: the trail guides, the cowboys, the ranch hands I met along the way, the horses, and the cattle. The McIntyre legacy will forever be a part of me.

Thank you to Julie Sturgeon for editing *Showdown*. You've made this journey a wonderful experience.

Thank you to my writing pals for brainstorming sessions and beta reading.

Thank you to Nan Rowe for helping me create another beautiful cover.

Thank you to my fellow writers for your support and friendship. Thanks to all who come to book signings, support me on social media, leave reviews, and encourage me to write the next book. Behind the solitary endeavor of writing, there's a village I'm truly grateful for.

Thank you to my family for the unconditional love and support. I love you to the moon and back!

Unbranded
(Montana Bred Series Book 1)

"…*Unbranded* by Linda Bradley is a story filled with emotion. The writing and character development…were beautifully done…you won't be disappointed."
—*Readers' Favorite, Five Star Review*

"The author writes a fluid story, with a lot of detail and description…All in all, this is another winner from author Linda Bradley."
—*InD'tale Magazine*

Reunion
(Montana Bred Series Book 2)

"*Reunion*…is a fantastic story…a beautiful book!"
—*Readers' Favorite, Five Star Review*

"This is a perfect book for a cold night, a fireplace, and a cup of tea."
—*Amazon Review*

"Heartfelt family saga continues…did not disappoint."
—*Amazon Review*

"…remind(s) you to live in the moment."
—*BookBub Review*

CHAPTER 1

D AD ONCE TOLD me cultivating the perfect day was like mining for Montana sapphires. They didn't float to the surface. They were buried, and the only way to expose one was to sift through the dirty work of the everyday grind.

My heart raced in the late summer sun. Light flickered through the shaggy pine boughs before the world opened up, and the ridge of Montana sage and wildflowers welcomed us. I eased Gypsy into a canter, the fringe of my chaps keeping time with her graceful strides.

Gypsy was more than a horse; she understood me better than anyone, and as long as I had her, I knew I wouldn't carry burdens alone.

The rosebush I'd planted in the clearing, next to the stone cross honoring my grandpa, was in full bloom. The sacred spot overlooked the 617 Ranch—6/17 marked my grandparents' wedding date. Winston and Ida May had built more than the McIntyre homestead—they'd built a legacy.

Nudging my cowboy hat back, I smiled at the

man I'd made a life with, my partner, the father of our fifteen-month-old twins, Lil and Gracie May. The man who believed marriage wasn't for everyone—just like me. Matt Cooper had my back, and I had his.

"I promise we'll have an all-girls day soon." I reined Gypsy in and stroked her dewy coat. She glanced back at me, the star on her ebony forehead as white as snow.

Matt snapped open a plaid blanket, made himself comfortable, and invited me to sit.

I dismounted, inhaling the fresh air. Gypsy lowered her head, sniffed Matt's hair, and batted her lashes at him until he fed her the carrot tucked in his shirt pocket.

"Flirt," I said.

"Who? Me or the horse you consider your soul sister?" Matt plucked a piece of wild grass and chewed on the stalky end.

I whispered sweet nothings to Gypsy. I loved her more than myself. She snatched a mouthful of greens before I tied her near Matt's horse, Trigger, who appeared to be enjoying an afternoon nap.

"I'm not some rattling snake or snarling bobcat, Momma. You weren't so shy last night. Come on, now." Matt patted the blanket.

"Last night was special. Candles. Music. Sleeping babies."

"Romance." His dimples framed his infectious smile.

"Things are going great. The sun is out. You've accepted Dad's offer as co-CEO. Dad approved my proposal for a barn renovation." I plunked myself down and fanned my cheeks.

"Yes, things are dandy." Matt ran his finger down my neck and across my collarbone. His gentle touch tickled, and it was all I could do to catch my breath as his fingers wiggled beneath my shirt and rested on my belly.

"I have a secret." I scooched around and sat knee-to-knee with him.

"Are you pregnant?" His face paled.

"No. The barn renovation is just the beginning. It'd be the perfect place for an idea I have."

"You know what would be more perfect?" Matt beckoned me closer.

"What?"

"If you'd kiss me. You can tell me about your idea later." He handed me a yellow rose.

"The last time you gave me one of Grandpa's roses, I ended up pregnant."

"And Lil and Gracie May are the perfect set of twins, despite the determined stubborn streak Gracie inherited from you."

"Yes, they are, and I'm sure you're right about the personality streak she will no doubt use to become a fine leader one day. Apples don't fall far from the tree. I'm a lot like my momma, too."

"Let's make today about us." He pressed his fingers to my lips. "On the count of three, we'll say what's in our hearts."

"Sounds like a risky game. I'm not exactly the gushy kind of gal."

"I'll take my chances." Matt raised one finger, then another, and another.

"I love our life just the way it is." I held his hands in mine and took in his dreamy gaze. "You didn't say anything."

"I didn't say anything on purpose."

"You tricked me. That wasn't—"

Matt put his fingers to my lips, again.

"I want to marry you."

When had his feelings changed about getting married? Hadn't he just agreed that everything was great between us?

"I know how you feel about getting hitched, and the word *marriage* scares the hell out of you, but things are changing. Your parents' divorce really did a number on you. My parents have been married for thirty-seven years and lived through some tough times. No marriage is perfect. Even

Maggie and your daddy have their moments. We've established a home together, a family."

The two-way radio I'd left in Gypsy's saddle-bag beeped.

"I should get that in case something's wrong."

Matt stood, helped me up, kissed me, then leaned against the boulder in the middle of the field. I answered the nanny's call and gazed into the lush green valley where my grandpa's White Park cattle grazed with the black Angus Matt owned.

"Hey, Maria. Is everything okay with the girls?"

"Yup. I'm just checking in before we go outside to play. Wanted you to know there was a call about a horse. The message is on the kitchen counter."

"Thanks. I'll be home soon." I tucked the yellow rose Matt had given me in my shirt pocket, took a deep breath, and pretended not to be fazed. "The girls are fine. You ready to go home, cowboy?"

"Yup." He tucked the blanket in one of Trigger's saddlebags.

I tugged the brim of my cowboy hat. He'd more than mentioned the word *marriage*, and Maria's timing couldn't have been better. I loosened Gypsy's reins from the branch and fed her an apple.

"What *is* he thinking?" Gypsy's ears twitched with my words. "Look at him. He's pretty pleased with himself. I bet he's just trying to get a rise out of me."

Matt untied Trigger, put his foot in the stirrup, and mounted his horse. I peered up at him.

"I *am* pleased, and I've been wanting to tell you how I feel for a long time. They say taking the first step is the hardest. You're the only woman for me, Chloe McIntyre."

I put my foot in the stirrup, grabbed the saddle horn, and pulled myself up. Gypsy stood nose to nose with Trigger. His chestnut coat was dotted with white spots.

"Did you really—" I held Matt's sparkling gaze.

"I sure did. I'm just giving you a head's up. The next time I mention it, I'll be prepared, get down on one knee, have a ring, and ask you the proper way."

"You're pulling my leg." I hunkered down in the saddle.

"You can believe what you want, but I'm giving you fair warning. No risk, no reward."

"What has gotten into you?"

"You have." Matt pointed Trigger toward the trail home. "Oh—Maggie's coming home today, and she's bringing a surprise."

CHAPTER 2

MAGGIE, MY STEPMOM, had complained about back pain last week. She'd spent more time grimacing than anything else until Dad took her to urgent care. After the attending physician sent her for imaging, she was admitted for surgery to remove a kidney stone blockage. She said the experience was more taxing than childbirth.

Maggie's mom, Glad, and I made and hung a homemade welcome home sign for Maggie in the foyer of the main house. Lil and Gracie had fallen asleep in the living room while listening to a recording of the tunes my dad sings around the evening bonfire. Toys littered the floor and our curious bulldog, Samson, had curled up in his tattered bed with a bone.

"Maggie is supposed to be here by now. I miss my girl. It's not the same when she's gone. I'll sleep better tonight," Glad said. "I know she'll be hungry." She pushed the blue speckled reading glasses perched at the end of her nose to the top of her head and stared out the kitchen window.

"I'm sure three Dutch ovens of chuck roast, potatoes, carrots, onions, and mushrooms will fill her up. You made enough for an army."

"And we've got one. Those wranglers need their meat and vegetables."

"There." I gestured to the kitchen island large enough for a family dinner, then draped my arm around Glad's thin eighty-nine-year-old shoulders and gave her a squeeze. "We're ready for huckleberry ice cream when she gets here."

Lil and Gracie's nanny, Maria, poked her head into the kitchen. Her brunette bob framed her dark eyes and button nose. "Is it okay if I head back to the house? There's laundry to fold and toys to pick up."

I nodded, then sniffed the bouquet of pink Chiffon roses Glad had arranged in a crystal vase. Their pedals were soft as silk and frillier than a ball gown.

"Call if you need me." Maria pointed out the kitchen window. "Looks like they're here. Matt says Maggie's bringing a surprise. *He* sure is handsome."

I peered over Glad's shoulder. Dad helped Maggie from the back seat of the SUV. Bradley, Maggie's only son, forty-one—soon to be forty-two, five days after my twenty-seventh birthday on August 22—unloaded the suitcases. His fiancée, Red, joined him at the rear of the truck. She was a head shorter than my six-foot-tall stepbrother. Her auburn hair cascaded down her back.

"Did you know they were coming?" I asked.

Glad clapped. "Good surprise, huh?"

I ran outside, threw my arms around Bradley, and kissed his cheek. "This beard is new—and scratchy. It's as red as your hair. Wow!"

"I like it," Red said, opening her arms. Glittering shards of light bounced from the round diamond solitaire on her ring finger.

"I'm so glad you're here." I squeezed Red tight. She felt thinner than last December, when they'd flown in to celebrate the twins' first Christmas.

"Guess having a little surgery is all it takes to get these two here." Maggie smiled.

"You must be feeling better if you're leading with a guilt trip. Your hospital stint is the perfect excuse for a few days off." Bradley grabbed a suitcase in each hand.

Glad stopped him at the front door, kissed him, and patted his cheeks. The gleam in her eye was one of pure love and joy. Next to Bradley, Glad appeared slight as ever. She'd claimed she'd been shrinking, and from where I stood, she had.

Bradley was broad-shouldered with the sweetest disposition. He towered over his nana. He loved sports, living in Boston, and being a lawyer. Since he'd met Red, she owned his heart.

Bradley and I were fifteen years apart in age and different in so many ways. He was a city boy, and I preferred the country. He'd once told me that when his mom had married my dad, he wasn't so sure about inheriting a pesty, strong-willed younger sister. It's twenty years later and I believe he still thinks I'm pesty and more strong-willed than ever, but in the loveliest of ways.

Bradley had been twenty-two when his parents split. His take on divorce differed from mine. He'd been hurt, too, but his parents had stayed together until he was an adult. I'd been a toddler when my mom and dad divorced. For me, this meant two houses, two sets of rules, and two parents who went from having everything in common to having only one thing in common—me.

When I was with my mother, her quiet jabs regarding my father weren't quiet at all. When I was with my father, his silence and rippling temple were a usual reaction when it came to dealing with my mother. As much as I idolized my mother's charisma and my father's loyalty to those he loved, I'd been caught in the middle. My parents lived life as if they'd never loved each other.

Bradley took the luggage upstairs to the guest room. Maggie, Glad, Red, and I moved to the kitchen after I checked on the girls. Lil was curled up with her blanket next to Gracie, who slept on her back, sprawled out like she'd been flattened in a cartoon.

Maggie fawned over the Chiffon roses, then sat at the counter and read the card. Glad scooped huckleberry ice cream.

"What's your recovery look like?" I pulled out a stool for Red.

"I won't be riding for a while, that's for sure. After I get the stent out at the end of next week, I'll have a better idea of what I can and shouldn't be doing. This is something I hope I never have to go through again."

"I had a friend who had kidney stone surgery and laid her kitchen floor a week later," Glad said.

"I won't be that girl." Maggie's brow dipped with the tone of her voice.

We sat around the kitchen island, gabbing about missed time together, until Glad asked Red if she and Bradley had started planning their wedding. They had agreed on a small ceremony with family, but not a date or destination. The animated excitement between Maggie and Glad pinged like a neon sign. I listened politely from the sidelines.

"You two should get married here." I licked my spoon clean and took in the stunned gazes.

Matt and Tristan sauntered in from the mudroom.

"The afternoon chores are done. Was wondering if your dad was free to catch up on the day." Matt took off his hat and Tristan followed suit.

Tristan had signed on with us just about the time I'd discovered I was pregnant with the twins. We'd had our scuffles to say the least. While proving myself to my father, I'd driven Tristan away, almost losing his brother Justin, my long-time friend, in the scrape. Tristan belonged here. This ranch was more than a home to Grandpa's eccentric white cattle; it attracted broken people like I collected horses who needed homes.

"You sure were up early this morning," Tristan said to me.

The heat rising in my cheeks would be a tell-all if I connected with Matt's smoldering expression. His soft whispers and hot kisses while entangled beneath the sheets were etched in my mind.

"The girls were fussing," Matt said.

"Wonder who they get that from?" Bradley joked. He cackled louder when Red pinched his bicep. "What? It's true."

"You sure you want to marry my brother?" My gaze met Red's.

"Come on, now. Don't be putting doubt into my girl's head," he retorted. "That's all you."

Before I could spout back, Matt tugged at my hand and pulled me from my stool.

"Nice boots, Chloe." Red's blue eyes sparkled as brightly as her engagement ring.

"Thanks, they're new," I said.

"What happened to the studded boots your mom sent before the girls were born?" Maggie finished her ice cream.

"As much as Mom would like me to wear those every day, I don't. When she was here a few weeks ago, we went boot shopping. This is the pair I settled on so I could save the others for special occasions—like not walking through muddy fields or manure and not mucking out stalls."

"You women and your boots and horses." Matt jumped back before I could swat him with the kitchen towel.

"Hey, now," Dad said, joining us. "That's no way to treat my new co-CEO."

"They're off the clock, and boots are serious business." Glad waggled her finger at Matt.

"Hey, John. Tristan and I were wondering if

you have a minute."

"Sure thing, son. My office in fifteen."

"Sounds good," Matt and Tristan said in unison.

I rinsed out my sticky bowl and put it in the dishwasher. Glad checked on dinner. Bradley raved about the aromas wafting through the kitchen. Maggie basked in the family gathering.

"That's enough food for a small army, Nana." Bradley took the silicone mitts from her and closed the oven door.

"Like I told Chloe"—she gestured to the kitchen full of people—"and this doesn't include the other three cowboys and Trout. I've still got it." Glad tapped her nose.

Matt and I excused ourselves, went outside, and walked to the creek.

"What's going on?" I bent down to touch the cool stream narrow enough to jump over without getting wet.

"Nothing. Just thought I'd take fifteen minutes to be with the momma of my girls. Spending time alone with you this morning was nice."

"Sure was." I picked up a flat stone marbled with reds and browns, then tucked it into my pocket. Bradley and Red's distant laughter cut the quiet between us.

"Let's check out the old barn." I had my own dreaming to do. "Oh, when you see my dad, can you *not* mention the horse I said I'd take in?"

"You're taking in another horse?" The corners of Matt's mouth drew down. "Pretty soon we'll have more horses than cows."

"Hardly." I rested my arms on his broad shoulders. "We make a good team."

"We make a *great* team. I meant what I said earlier about wanting to marry you."

"I think Bradley and Red are getting to you. It's easy to want what others have."

"I know what I want, and I want you, Momma." Matt winked.

Lola, the rescue sheltie mix Matt adopted to work the cattle, greeted us as we walked toward the barn.

"If you listen hard enough, I can hear boot heels in the loft overhead, music, and the laughter of happy partygoers. Sometimes, I hear soft voices of those who need time alone after bonding with the animals. This barn can bring people together like it did when my grandparents were newly married. We're surrounded by potential."

Lola flushed the barn cat, Coal, from the shadows of an empty stall and chased her upstairs. Matt and I followed. I turned on the bare bulb hanging above the landing. Coal scampered into a dark corner of the loft and reappeared with a mouse between her teeth.

"She brought you a present," Matt said.

"It's the thought that counts. No thanks." I shooed her away.

"Shall we dance?" Matt took me in his arms.

Lola barked. She wagged her tail, her dark gaze intrigued. Matt hummed a romantic tune, and we waltzed.

"I think Lola wants to cut in," I said.

"She can cut in another time." Matt tossed her a jerky treat from his pocket. With a snap of her head, she caught it mid-air, ate it, and trotted downstairs.

"Matt, when did you change your mind about getting married?"

"I've been feeling it for a while now. Let's just keep dancing." He finished his song, then answered Dad's call on the radio.

Ribbons of sunlight warmed my cheeks as I stared out the loft window. I'd stood here many times before. I felt the slightest of wedges forming, and I wondered if Matt could feel it, too. He was raising the stakes, and I'd need my cowgirl grit to handle the situation without upsetting the balance he and I had achieved, all without saying *I do*.

CHAPTER 3

THE LULL OF the creaking antique rocker drifted into the crevices of midnight as I rocked Lillian. Ida May had used this chair to soothe my dad when he was a baby, and it had become part of my ritual too. Gracie had cut a tooth last week, which meant it was Lil's turn, and she was right on schedule.

Gracie crawled first, then Lil. Gracie stood, danced like a marionette with buckling knees. Lil followed a week later. When Gracie took her first steps, Lil grimaced, then sat back down in protest as if she knew she didn't want to grow up.

"You gonna follow in your sister's footsteps all your life?"

Lil stared at me with big eyes. The crease in her brow seemed apologetic.

"I know, little girl. You don't have to keep up with your sister or anyone else. And if I had a wand, I'd make the hurt disappear. Actually, I'd change lots of things. I don't want anything to come between us, especially divorce. And you can't get divorced if you don't get married."

Lil's eyes glistened in the moonlight. "You always look so serious." She wrapped her tiny fingers around mine. She was perfect even if my realistic nature warned me no one was, most of all me.

Thoughts of Red and Bradley's wedding busied my mind.

"You gonna stay in here all night, Momma?" Matt touched my shoulder.

"Guess I got lost in a daydream."

I handed him Lil. Her eyelids fluttered, and we waited for her to settle. The scents of baby powder and shampoo reminded me of everything brand-new and innocent.

Matt tiptoed across the room to the crib. His love for our daughters melted my heart. While he tucked Lil beneath her downy blanket, I wished upon the Montana moon.

"Come on, Chloe."

I laced my fingers with his and squeezed just as Lil had done to me before falling asleep. I figured she'd be holding on to me and her daddy for most of her life.

"Goodnight, sweet girls." I blew them a kiss and left the door ajar.

"It's so peaceful when they're sleeping," Matt

said, leading me to bed.

"I can't wait until the girls are old enough to ride."

"All in due time. Let's not rush things."

"Exactly." My reply was more poignant than I expected. Disappointment seemed to cloud his gaze. My belly dipped with what I interpreted as hurt.

Matt crawled beneath the covers, his thick dark messy hair like a young boy without a care in the world. I inspected the whiskers on his chin.

"I like your long hair and scruff."

"I heard chicks dig this look," he mumbled, his sleepy eyes closed.

Moonlight upon the ceiling stirred enchanted visions of a white buttercream wedding cake, lacy shoes, and bouquets of wildflowers. Matt rolled over on his side and peered at me from beneath his dark lashes.

"Oh boy," he said.

"What?" I pretended not to know one of his strengths was reading my mind. I drew the sheet up to my chin, tossed and turned, then fluffed the pillow—the pillowcase cool against my cheek. Not dwelling on Matt's proposal was getting the best of me.

"Dang, girl. I don't know who's worse. You or

Lola."

"Nothing wrong with getting as comfortable as I can."

"Thought you didn't believe in getting comfortable. Thought you believed having an edge keeps emotion at bay."

"It's how I'm built. And, last time I checked, we agreed on loving life together without paperwork and wedding rings. What made you change your mind?"

When my parents split, so many things went wrong, and it seemed to me that when I let down my guard, heartache was inevitable. Broken promises and resentment led to a rocky long-distance relationship with my Hollywood fashionista mom, being raised by my father, and two parents who couldn't stand each other.

Sometimes, I wished I weren't hard around the edges, but I didn't know how to soften. I'd spent most my life with my dad, my grandfather, the wranglers, and Trout—the ranch's former foreman—and Maggie who always found the bright side, a quality only time could season. Trusting myself to feel deeper evoked an unfathomable risk, and the consequences of my parents' divorce warranted self-protection.

"You never know what tomorrow will bring,"

Matt said. He stroked my cheek, and my heart pinched. Everyone had their hurt, including the man lying by my side.

He traced my collarbone with his callused finger. Matt knew me better than I knew myself.

"Grandpa's roses are so beautiful." I reached over to the nightstand and fingered the yellow rose Matt had given me.

"You're like those flowers and your grand-dad...a force to be reckoned with, the foundation that makes this ranch breathtaking and hearty."

Afraid to lose the moment between us, I held his gaze. His well of patience for me was endless.

"You have to peel away those layers guarding your heart. Sometimes, hurt reaps the biggest crops."

"If that's your way of telling me it's good to fall down, I'd rather not. I prefer walking by your side without taking chances."

"Scars remind us we lived."

"I don't like scars." I rolled onto my back and stared at the ceiling.

"Worrying about the future won't do any good." Matt kissed my cheek. "Chloe?"

"Yeah, cowboy."

"Do us all a favor and don't borrow trouble. And I'm more than a cowboy, I'm the man who wants to spend all his days as your husband."

"Someday, none of us will be here." Who would be sleeping in this room, running this ranch? I prayed Lil and Gracie would love this Montana home as much as I did and they'd keep it alive. I don't know what made me think of the ranch without Dad, Maggie, Glad, Matt, Trout, and the wranglers who'd become family. Loss was inevitable, and I wouldn't lose anyone on my watch.

"That's a cheery thought. Not." Matt turned off the lamp on the nightstand.

I kicked off the covers, put on my slippers, then tripped over the upholstered bench at the end of the bed.

"Where are you going?" He propped himself up on bent elbows.

"There's a wedding to plan. I'll be in my office." I sat at the edge of the bed next to Matt. Planning a wedding wasn't the only task on my agenda.

"Bradley and Red haven't even decided where they're gonna get married."

"You didn't see the light in Red's eyes when I mentioned it. I'm sure they'll get hitched here. Go to sleep. I promise I won't stay up all night."

"Taking the attention away from us won't

change my feelings, Chloe."

"Like you said, you don't know what tomorrow will bring, and I want to be prepared. I know you think I'm being my usual self." I ran my fingers through Matt's mane. He pulled me close, and I kissed him. "In the end, all that will matter is that we loved each other."

CHAPTER 4

MORNING LIGHT CREPT from beneath the cloak of night's darkness, unveiling the majestic Montana landscape. The horses roamed the hillside, waiting for their escort home. The view from my office never disappointed.

I'd already eaten my usual oatmeal with sliced banana and was out the door when Maria arrived.

I'd been waking up before the crack of dawn since I was a kid. Morning fog and chilly air ushered in a new day. The late-night conversation I had with Matt was still fresh in my mind. I'd combed the internet for wedding ideas, bookmarked flower arrangements, menus, and flower girl dresses for Lil and Gracie.

Borrowing trouble, as Matt called it, wasn't something I did to purposely ruffle feathers or avoid the obvious. Living my grandparents' legacy meant passing on something to my girls that wouldn't just keep Winston and Ida May's spirits alive—it'd encompass those of us who came after and our riffs on the importance of cattle and horses.

I rode Gypsy up the hillside and kept Tristan and Matt in sight from a fair distance. Static filled the airwaves from the two-way radio. A hitch of panic curdled my blood. Things were different now. Every call scraped my nerves at the least expected times, even though I knew my daughters were in good hands.

Maria had lost her father to lung cancer and quit school to care for him so her mother could continue working. She'd said maintaining a routine helped with the grief.

I lucked out when Maria Santos came into our lives.

I also knew Maria wouldn't be with us long-term, as much as I wanted her to be. She had her sights set on graduating with a degree in early education. We'd had many conversations about children, their emotional needs, play, and learning. She was more than a nanny; she was a support system. I'd heard Glad say, *it takes a village* on more than one occasion, which made me think it was time to expand the definition of ranching.

"Chloe, you there?" Tristan's voice boomed over the radio speaker. "I don't see you."

"I'm in the pines looking for Huckleberry and Hitchcock. I'll be down in a few minutes. Keep the line open."

"Copy."

Wispy pine needles brushed against my neck as I rode farther up the incline.

"You got those two vigilantes?"

"I see them."

"Get a move on. Maggie's got breakfast waiting for us."

"I'll be there in a minute." Gray clouds rolled in, and light rain fell from the brim of my hat. "Come on, Gypsy, let's get these two." I leaned forward with the incline, trying to ease her load. "I swear, you're the only one who never bucks my system."

Gypsy lost her footing on the slick ground. "Careful, girl."

Huckleberry, who didn't seem to have a care in the world, perked up when I whistled. Hitchcock sauntered past and headed toward the herd, waiting to run home. Gypsy tripped again, this time almost toppling over. Her whinny cut the mist, and Huckleberry bolted.

"That's one way to get her going. The cows won't wait forever." Gypsy and I got our bearings and headed down the hillside, too.

The rolling clouds had stolen the golden sunrise. The sky threatened a downpour, and as much as I didn't mind riding in the water and mud, my stomach growled for Maggie's homemade pancakes.

I zipped my jacket to keep the rain off my neck. Tristan waved at me to hurry. His patience with horses exceeded his patience with people.

Trout manned the gate and eyed the herd eager to run. His white moustache characterized his burly disposition.

Trout had worked the ranch since Dad was knee-high. Trout was more than a hired hand; he was my granddad's best friend. He was family. When he stepped down, I became foreman. But his idea of stepping down didn't mean retire by any means. He was pure cowboy and was born to work the herds.

He'd settled into his renovated timber cabin on the river, rekindled the flame with his long-lost love, Hermione Crow, and declared seventy-eight the new fifty. He'd be riding until the bitter end.

When Trout opened the gate and the horses sprinted for the corral, Gypsy and I brought up the rear until I nudged her with my heels. Taking the lead and riding like thunder came natural to both of us.

Maggie leaned against the barn door, watching the horses file into the corral. She coveted the morning ritual as much as I did. Her pleased expression was one of joy even if she wasn't feeling 100 percent. Fifty horses made for a majestic sight when given the opportunity to run.

She drew the collar of her coat closed, and my stare was riveted to her wedding ring. A shiver ran down my spine. I doubted it was the Montana chill.

I called Tristan on the radio. "The horses are secure in the corral. Bring in Boomerang."

Tristan had acquired the mare from his Wyoming friend, Branch Sims. I wasn't the only one willing to take on a horse in need, and Branch always seemed to have a wild one for Tristan.

Boomerang's blue eyes reflected her wild spirit, her shiny coat black as night. Tristan stayed with her, his serious stare distraction-free. As usual, it was him and his newest conquest against the world. Boomerang ran into the empty field adjacent the corral. She kicked and snapped her head from side to side.

"Don't give me that look," he said, trotting by.

"Who? Me or Boomerang?"

"Both of you." Tristan's hard words matched his gaze. He rode into the pasture ready to quiet the unsettled, and I dismounted Gypsy and closed the gate behind him. The man's blood ran deep and calm for the unbroken.

Trout rode in and dismounted. "That young man just keeps getting better."

Gypsy sniffed Trout, then rested her chin on his shoulder. Gypsy had once been a handful, too.

I admired Trout's calm demeanor and stern disposition. He commanded respect effortlessly. Trout narrowed his distinguished gaze and studied Tristan, then glanced my way.

"What's wrong with you, girl?"

"I was thinking there's more to this place than breeding cattle and raising horses. People come with baggage. These animals always have a listening ear when it came to my worries. There's something to tap into, and I think my grandparents would agree."

Maggie leaned on the fence rail and rested her chin on her hands. The gold flecks in her green eyes shimmered like the misty sprinkles of rain dancing in the early morning light.

"Your dad's set in his ways," she said. "The barn renovation is one thing. I don't suppose you've told him about this other idea."

"Not yet. Matt doesn't know either."

Dad didn't like change any more than I did, especially when it came with a price tag. Getting him to approve the barn reno had been difficult— getting him to agree to opening a therapy center would be a monumental feat.

"Tristan would be a great asset," I said, watching him work Boomerang. Gypsy shook her head, then put her ears back. Tristan's wife, Vivian, and son, James, were killed in an accident when a semitruck had crossed the double yellow lines in broad daylight. Tristan wrangled more than the animals. "We could help so many children."

"That's your heart speaking. Grand ideas come to those who fall in love with the land." Trout clicked his tongue against his teeth.

Montana love was unyielding and loyal. It grabbed my dad by the hand when he was a youngster and never let go. It was in my genes, too, and I belonged here more than anywhere else on this earth. Maggie's tender stare tugged at my heart.

"You feeling okay, Maggie?"

"Feeling just fine."

Lola ran under the fence rail and circled the group of horses in the corral Boomerang eyed from the adjacent pasture.

Tristan dismounted Casanova, took the rope from his saddle, and stepped closer to Boomerang. Her skittish attitude held everyone's attention. Lola did her job, and Tristan did his. The breeze prickled the hair on the nape of my neck, and I swore I heard a boy—I wanted to believe was Tristan's son—say, *Get 'em, Dad.*

I wrapped my arm under Gypsy's neck, held her close. Everyone deserved a horse's friendship. Tristan's unwavering presence grew stronger. He was a man unwilling to take no for an answer.

And, I, Chloe McIntyre, daughter of John and granddaughter of Winston Ludlow and Ida May, knew something about an unwavering mindset, too. I hadn't added marriage to my bucket list with good reason. And now that Matt wanted to get married, I realized there was more to protect than myself.

I tied Gypsy to the hitching post and went into the barn. The aroma of coffee lingered in the nook we used for an office. I closed the door behind me, took the note from my pocket, and dialed the number for the man with the pinto that needed a home.

"Hi, this is Chloe McIntyre. Hope I'm not calling too early."

"Nope. Not at all. You ready to pick up Rosie?" There was a hitch in his voice.

"Is there a problem? Did someone else speak for her?"

"Quite the opposite. The young lady who'd spoken for the other pinto, Blue, has changed her mind."

"I'll take her, too." I ignored the dip in my belly.

"You sure?"

"You said, they're both gentle souls, and that's exactly what I'm looking for. I'll get in touch with Doc Neely's office and we'll be out." I said goodbye and hung up the phone. I took in the black-and-white photos of my grandparents lining the walls. I stood, pushed back my shoulders. They'd approve.

Matt poked his head into the office, reminding me about breakfast.

"I'll be along in a minute."

"You okay, Momma?"

"Yeah. Sometimes doing the right thing is hard." I tucked the man's name and number in my pocket.

"Those pancakes and maple sausages won't stay warm forever." Matt put his arm around my shoulders and ushered me outside. "You wanna talk about it?"

"No," I said.

"I know doing the right thing may feel prickly, but you have to follow your heart."

"Definitely." Exchanging smiles lifted my spirits.

The sunshine had chased the last clouds away.

The warm light washed over me like the sign I awaited. I shoved my hands in my jean pockets and rubbed the miniature horseshoe Matt had given me when the girls began teething. I was a sucker for a good luck charm.

CHAPTER 5

After breakfast, I slipped away from the wrangling crew and the north pasture of grazing cattle. I'd have to tell my dad about the two pintos I knew would pass the vet's exam and join the herd. A lone cricket serenaded me as the toes of my boots met the creek's pebbly edge. I kneeled, then skimmed the cool water with the palm of my hand.

The rain had washed away the hesitation I'd held onto when it came to telling my father I wanted to use horses to help people. Meeting and spending time with our vet's twelve-year-old daughter, Emma, validated the need for this community service. She was withdrawn and talked little for a girl on the cusp of being a teenager. When she connected with the horses the weight she carried seemed to ease.

Dad's touch on my shoulder was something I always welcomed.

"Hi." I stood.

"You're mighty distracted." He drew me close.

"I'm betting you don't want to talk about it. I'll find out soon enough. There's usually a phone call. I don't need to remind you that we said we'd be forthright when it came to business." The corners of his mouth drew down. "Is everything okay between you and Matt?"

I took a deep breath. "I'm bringing two new horses to the ranch. Found them through Doc Neely. He'll examine them this afternoon." I faced my father.

He rubbed his whiskery chin. "Focusing your energy on a new project won't ease what's eating at you. Taking the bull by the horns can also be mighty liberating."

"Emotions are hard." I held his stare, hoping he could read my mind. "Just to be clear, it's not a project, it's projects."

"Working out your frustrations through the animals has always been a good outlet. Moving here was the one thing your mother and I agreed upon. She knew we both belonged here before I did."

I reciprocated Dad's easy smile. City living as a pediatrician had called to my father as a young man, and Grandpa's invitation home to help with the White Park catered to the ache my dad had for his family's ranch. When I finished second grade, we moved here. Dad and my mother knew it was my future. And now my daughters'.

"Must've been hard having such different dreams," I said.

"And then you came along."

"Lucky for you." I couldn't help but laugh. Dad hugged me tight.

"You'll always be my Paris girl."

"I love you and Mom so much. I was a fool to believe she didn't want me with her while I was growing up."

"Not a fool." He took my hand in his. "We all have misconceptions."

"Like the one you have about me growing out of taking in homeless horses."

"Yes. But I suppose I'll get over it like I always do."

"Great. While we're on an upswing, I want to open a therapy center and use the horses to help others."

"We can't house a therapy center. We're not set up for that. Far from it, and the barn reno is expensive. We've got our hands full finding homes for the horses we already have. And we've got two more on the way."

"Have I ever brought one home that's danger-ous, sick, or lame?"

"No. I can't say that you have. Suppose that's why it's so hard to get rid of them. They're easy to get attached to."

"Did you ever think it's easier to talk to your horse than a human?" I lowered my chin.

"Yep." Dad sighed and rubbed away the pinch between his brows. "I've done my fair share of talking to the animals, too."

"When the vet comes out, watch her daughter, Emma. She's so quiet, and she has little communication until she connects with the horses. I'm sure there are lots of children who could use an outlet."

Dad groaned.

"When I see the sadness in Emma's eyes, I want to help."

"Lil and Grace are making you soft." The corner of his mouth curled. "Look, Sarah's daughter is a sweet girl. Not all children are talkers like you."

"Touché, and the girls are hardly making me soft. This ranch is their future, too."

"As much as I'd like to get on board with your idea. I can't. The cattle Matt's added to the herd are multiplying, and you've got your horses. It's not in the cards. Let's get the barn done. Have the shindig you've been dreaming of and move forward. I'm not getting any younger."

"Neither am I." I held his gaze. "Finding homes for the horses would be a good place to start. Right? It'd free up some of the budget."

"Chloe—" The tone of his voice dipped.

I shoved my hands in my pockets and rubbed the miniature horseshoe. "Working on the barn with Mr. Featherstone isn't exactly a distraction. He's a fabulous architect." Working on the barn fueled my intentions.

"When you're ready to tell me what's brewing between you and Matt, you know where to find me." Dad pushed his shoulders back, tucked his thumbs in his belt loops, and scanned the horizon.

"Dang."

"I said I'd stay out of your personal life, and I will, but I can see it in your eyes when you look at that boy. Life is hard enough. I know Maggie and Glad are your go-tos, but I'm here for you."

"Thanks, Dad. Matt and I are fine. I just wonder what he's thinking sometimes."

"It's pretty clear to me."

It was pretty clear to me, too, and it wasn't what we agreed to.

"Are we good here?" Dad tugged the brim of his hat.

"Yes, Dad. Can you let the guys know I'll catch up with them later? I've got calls to make." I took in his scowl. "What's with the look? If you must know, there's a guy interested in Sway and Domino. I should follow through. You like that sort of initiative, remember?"

"Who's the guy?"

"His name is Dennis. He's the husband of one of Glad's friends from the women's club. Says he lost a bet with his wife and now owes their daughters some easy riders. You're gonna ask Glad, aren't you?"

"Not right now. We've got work to do. And, you can tell the guys you'll catch up later. I've got something I need to take care of myself."

I hopped over the creek and headed to the barn.

Silas, the Pied Piper of the work crew, tinkered with Grandpa's vintage pickup truck. We hit pay dirt when we hired him. He was a jack-of-all-trades, big as the lumberjack with the blue ox in the fairy tale books, sang to the animals, and was sweet as berry jam. Lil and Grace loved him as much as the rest of us. Those two were like a couple of hounds when it came to sniffing out good people.

"Hey, Silas." I walked past at a decent clip.

"Hey, back." He shut the hood of the truck and wiped his hands on the bandanna from his back pocket. "Looks like someone's in a hurry."

"Got phone calls to make. I'll be in the office. Could you let Matt and Tristan know they can ride out to the pasture without me? I'll catch up later."

"Sure thing. But they won't like being a man short."

"Thanks, Silas. You're the best." I went into the barn office and shut the door behind me to search for Dennis's number I'd crumpled up and thrown away last night. Suddenly, I heard Matt talking to Tristan outside the door. I kicked the empty can under the desk.

"Shoot, I'll have to ask Glad for his number," I said to myself as I opened the door.

"Howdy, bosslady." Matt smiled.

"Not so sure I'm the bosslady to you anymore now that you're the co-CEO."

"You're looking a little flushed. Do you feel okay?"

"I'm great."

"Your dad said Sway and Domino might be getting a new home."

"Where'd you come from?" I raised my brow.

"I was at the main house helping Maggie move a table she needed for one of her projects. She's got a ton of photos. People sure do like her coffee table books."

"She's amazing. Says she's working on another one. Can't wait to see it." I tucked my fingers in my back pockets.

Matt took a wrinkled piece of paper from his shirt pocket and handed it to me.

"Guess you had words with my dad, too?"

"Enough to know that you'll be needing this right about now. I found it on the floor this morning after taking out the trash. You're a lousy shot."

I snatched the paper from him.

"He mentioned the horses you called about. I'd appreciate not getting in the middle."

"Sure thing." I winked.

"You weren't gonna call this guy, were you?"

I sighed.

"I'm glad you changed your mind. We can't keep them all."

"They really are sweet souls."

"You say that about *all* the horses."

"Not exactly. Tristan's brought some zingers. You see that one." I pointed out the window to the pasture adjacent to the corral. "Not so sweet."

"When Tristan gets done with Boomerang, she will be."

"You're probably right." I smoothed out the pink note paper. "I should call. I'll ride out to the pasture after I check in with Maria."

"I'll see you later." Matt rested his hand on the doorjamb. "Your dad also mentioned you told him about using the horses as therapy animals. Finding Sway and Domino a home will barely make a dent in what you think will make your dad change his mind. We'll still be at fifty."

"It's a start."

"Your dad won't change his mind."

"I told him I'd find these horses a home."

"If they need transport, let me know."

"Thanks. And—Matt."

"Yeah."

"I'm doing the best I can." I hoped he knew I was talking about more than horses.

CHAPTER 6

I'D COME IN from the pasture early, groomed Gypsy, and met Dad in the drive. Mr. Featherstone showed on time and brought his partner, Mr. Cortright. Mr. Featherstone was a tall, soft-spoken man, wearing a bull hide cowboy hat. His pinstraight black ponytail fell to the middle of his back. The silver feather charm on his hatband reminded me of the crow I'd nursed back to health as a child. Mr. Cortright, about Mr. Featherstone's height, wore jeans and a white tee. He opened his notepad and took the pen from his pocket.

I showed Mr. Featherstone and Mr. Cortright the first floor of the barn, which wasn't much more than a couple of stalls, a dowelled wall full of old horseshoes, and outdated tack. We climbed the staircase at the rear of Grandpa's barn. My nerves prickled with excitement. The renovation was happening.

Dust crowded the corners of each step. A haze of floating particles drifted in the light at the far end of the spacious loft. They twisted and flitted like pixie dust, mere remnants of the stories I'd told myself about Winston and Ida May.

"Chloe," Dad said, his hand on my arm. "What do you think?"

The faint vision of cowboy boots and a vintage dress crossed my mind. "Sorry? I tuned out for a second." I fiddled with the rim of my cowboy hat.

"This light is tremendous." Mr. Featherstone walked the room. "We could have this done in eight weeks." He made more notes. "This place has great possibilities. We'd redo the old stalls with repurposed materials. There's room for two more in the space where there's nothing but wasted space near the shoeing area—even make a tack room and a small bathroom." He flicked on his flashlight to inspect the timbers overhead. "These look solid. Up here, we could refinish the wood, replacing questionable floorboards, update the electricity. This would be a great meeting room."

"Exactly." Dad's sturdy frame absorbed my nudge. "I agree. This loft could be a multipurpose room for the therapy center and a meeting room for the wranglers."

"It would be the perfect place for a wedding," Dad said under his breath.

"I agree. That's why I mentioned it to Bradley and Red." Heat rose to my cheeks, and I walked to the opposite end of the room.

"We could install ceiling fans, furnish it, make it a place for solitude. Bookshelves filled with classics. Silas would love that. He's our wrangler litterateur." I could see myself reading, the girls playing with each other or sacking out on a cushy sofa after a long ride, and children having a snack after buddying up with a horse to talk to or care for.

"How would you feel about skylights?" Mr. Featherstone caught my father's gaze.

Dad paced. I knew he contemplated the budget. I also knew he loved stargazing as much as the rest of us. He scanned the room as if he were recalling childhood memories.

"Furniture would make it quite the space." Mr. Featherstone shared his notes with Mr. Cortright.

"We do have a faux bear rug that needs a home." I winked at my dad. "Mom knows it's going. She agrees her extravagant gift with the frightening stare was a decorating mistake."

"Last time I spoke to Antique Annie, she tried to sell me a couple of saddled barstools. Wonder if she still has them? I've got her on speed dial." Mr. Cortright pulled out his phone and excused himself.

"It'll be a great place to display the family

memorabilia. Horseshoes, branding irons, ropes, saddles, some of my grandparents' antiques." The hair stood up on the nape of my neck.

"Your daughter has great ideas." Mr. Cortright paced off the dimensions after ending his call and wrote them down. "It's plenty big enough."

The crows' feet at the corners of Mr. Featherstone's eyes were telling, his smile kind. Dad crossed his arms. He cradled the same pride I carried in my shoulders.

"I'll get back to you with a cost for skylights," Mr. Featherstone said.

"I'll take this for safekeeping." From the wall, I took the black-and-white photo of the land the way it looked when Grandpa and Grandma purchased it. The players may have changed, but we were all bred from the same heart.

Mr. Cortright ran his hand over the heavy half wall at the top of the stairs. "We can probably add a few touches you haven't thought of."

"I'd say skylights would tick that box." I wiggled my brows at Dad. Money should have been first and foremost in my mind, but this place had multipurpose written all over it.

"We'll generate numbers. Expect some drawings. The decision is yours," Mr. Cortright said.

"Thank you. I think I'm more excited about

getting this project started than anyone," I replied.

Mr. Featherstone, Mr. Cortright, and my dad went downstairs. I lagged behind, stealing an extra moment in the quiet room I envisioned. A cigar box tucked beneath a saddle in the far corner caught my attention. The cracked lid didn't take away from the charm of finding a treasure. The men's voices drifted up the stairwell as they noted the width of the staircase and number of risers.

Dad told Mr. Featherstone and Mr. Cortright that I'd stay up there all day if I could, and he was right. I turned off the light and went downstairs.

"Watcha got there?" Dad raised an eyebrow at me as he tucked his fingers into the back pockets of his faded jeans.

"A cigar box. I can't wait to see what's inside." I shook it, imagining the contents.

"Thanks again for making the trek out. I'm looking forward to revitalizing this place." Dad showed the men to their truck.

"You sure do have a beautiful place here." Mr. Featherstone gave me an affirmative nod, his dark stare captivating.

"We're pretty proud of it." Dad rested his hand on the back of my neck. My grin spread like wildfire.

"Your daughter reminds me of another blonde

with fire in her eyes," Mr. Featherstone said.

"Who's that?" I asked.

"Your grandmother, Ida May."

"You knew her?"

"Ida May and my mother were great friends since childhood. My mother told stories of a tenacious girl who loved my mother's tales of the mountains and animals. My mother once said that Ida May possessed the strength of all the mountains, and when she crumbled, she'd brush off the dust with great pride, only to rise again."

"I wish my mom could've lived to see this place now," Dad said.

The glint in his eye sent a chill down my spine.

"Your granddad wasn't the only one with ranching in his blood." Mr. Featherstone smiled.

Trout rode in on his best horse, Tupelo Honey. Her rich golden gaze was as sweet as the honey she was named after. Trout dismounted and shook hands with our visitors.

Before the girls were born, Mr. Featherstone had facilitated the move of Trout's family Virginia cabin to the ranch, then oversaw the rebuild and renovation. Trout's rustic home filled with his family history was magazine perfect, and I had no doubt Mr. Featherstone would transform my grandparents' barn into a beautiful, functional workspace, too.

"You still loving the cabin?" Mr. Featherston asked.

"One of the best decisions I ever made."

"Good for you." Mr. Cortright tucked his pen in his shirt pocket. "I hear you and Hermione are back together. Funny how life works out."

"Yup. When she showed up last year, she made my life. Now, when she leaves, I know she's coming back. Couldn't be happier." The apples of Trout's cheeks turned a rosy red and his bushy moustache had no chance at hiding his smile.

"You'll still be the cranky cowboy who was sent here to watch over me," I said.

The men talked until Mr. Cortright and Mr. Featherstone said their goodbyes. They waved from the truck's open windows before driving away.

I dug in my pocket for a piece of sugar for Tupelo.

"Don't go spoiling my horse," Trout said.

I ignored him and offered Tupelo the treat.

"That's how she gets you. She offers up the sweets then reels you in, and there ain't no release," Dad said.

"She never did play fair." Trout snickered.

"I learned it from the best, right, Dad? It's the

McIntyre way."

"Whatcha got there?" Trout asked.

"Not sure. I found it upstairs." Curiosity gnawed at my patience as I fiddled with the cigar box latch. Matt and Tristan rode in side by side on their favorite rides, with Justin, Silas, and Quinn behind.

"Everything okay with my cattle?" I asked.

"Doing fine. No casualties after rounding up strays. We could've used you out there." Matt paused. "The Angus I've added sure like it here."

"Yeah, bosslady. Hope you make time for us tomorrow. Someone needs to keep Tristan in line." Justin leaned into his saddle horn.

"You wish." Tristan galloped away.

Maggie's voice came over the two-way radio.

I answered, "Hey, Maggie."

"When the men leave, can you come up to the house?"

"Yeah, be there in a few. Are the girls okay? Is Maria there?"

"Yes and yes." She ended the call.

I shook the radio. It was unlike Maggie to cut me off. A motherly twinge of worry festered as I imagined goose-egged foreheads and pinched fingers.

"What's going on?" Matt slouched in his saddle and lowered his brows.

"Not sure. Maggie sounds fishy."

"You want me to go? If you need to talk to your dad, I'd be happy to."

"I got it. I think Dad and I are done here for today. Dad?"

"Go ahead, sugar bee."

I crinkled my nose at him. "*Sugar bee*? What's that all about?"

"That was your granddaddy's nickname for your grandmother. She was usually busier than a bee, getting things accomplished, and boy, could she sweet-talk her way through a sticky situation."

"Sounds like she's got one up on me there." I glanced at Justin. "I see your smirk."

He put his hands up and laughed behind his crooked smile. "Seriously, we needed your sass out there till the bitter end. Tristan's so distracted he wouldn't see a freight train coming."

"You two can spar later," Dad said, sending me on my way.

"I'll talk to him." With the cigar box in hand, I hurried to the main house. Taking a minute outside the mudroom door, I unlatched the box and peeked inside at the envelopes tied with a faded turquoise ribbon. Cursive scrawl piqued my interest, and I couldn't wait to inspect the contents.

CHAPTER 7

Maggie, Glad, Maria, Red, and the girls huddled around the dining room table set with girly plastic teacups and saucers. Red held a plate of sandwiches just the right size for two growing girls with enough teeth to manage.

"What do you have there, Chloe?" Maggie chose a sandwich with an extended pinky, then set it on her plate. "Dainty sandwiches require proper handling."

"Mine." Gracie reached for Maggie's sandwich.

Red touched her hand and showed her the plate filled with miniature peanut butter and jelly triangles. "That's Grandma Maggie's." Red lowered her gaze, and Gracie scowled.

"Listen to Red." I placed the box on the table. Gracie reached for me as I took a sandwich from the platter and handed it to her. "This one has your name on it. Looks yummy."

Gracie inspected the sandwich with her tiny fingers and astonished gaze. Instead of taking the sandwich, Gracie knocked the cigar box off the table. With a clunk, the lid popped open, and the contents spilled across the floor. Gracie clapped.

A delicate horseshoe, no bigger than a tree frog slipped out of an envelope. A silky ribbon the color of sapphires was tied neatly around it with a note attached. It was from Grandpa.

Dear Ida May – With any luck, we'll be proud ranch owners by the end of the week.

I turned the card over. Grandma had written a reply. *Swell, because John Patrick has outgrown the tiny house we're renting. The boy needs room to run and animals to keep him company. Love, Ida May.*

"Exactly." I picked up the letters and trinkets and gave Maggie the horseshoe. She read the note aloud, then popped a sandwich in her mouth.

"Guess I'm not the only one with lucky charms." I showed Maggie the miniature horseshoe from my pocket, then put it away before Gracie could snatch it.

Maggie returned the silver horseshoe to the cigar box.

"Funny how things appear after people say their goodbyes. Kind of like their way of saying, *we're still here.*" I put the letters back into the box, then closed the lid.

"You gonna read the letters?" Red bounced Lil on her knee.

"Absolutely."

"Sounds romantic." Maria clinked her cup to Gracie's.

"Bet there are some special ones in there. Probably a secret or two," Maggie whispered.

"I like a good secret." I plopped a tea sandwich into my mouth, then reached for another. Red stared at me as if she were a million miles away. "Bet you and Bradley have secrets, huh?"

"I suppose we do."

"Those kinds of secrets are golden." Maggie patted Red's hand.

"Being part of this family sure is nice." Red tickled Lil's chin.

"We like it, too. So glad we have a brood of girls to keep those men in their places." I ate another sandwich.

After the tea party, we decided a walk would do us all good before the girls went down for their afternoon nap. Maria and I got Lil and Gracie situated in the wagon we'd named Ranger and walked toward the barns. Along the way, the girls pointed out the house, truck, tree, horse, Momma, and bird. Their simple speech patterns were bound to turn into complex conversation in a blink of an eye.

Gracie stood up, and I stopped the wagon. She climbed out, and Maria took her hand. Gracie toddled into the grass.

"Flower." Gracie picked a daisy, then wanted back into the wagon.

Maria helped her get seated, then picked another daisy for Lil. Lil kissed her sister's hand and threw an invisible smooch to Maria. Maria returned the animated gesture.

"You know you can't ever leave us," I said.

Maria's cheeks blossomed with rosy emotion. She was the humblest person I'd met in a long time. She was as precious as a Montana sapphire, and I'd do anything to keep her as long as I could.

"She's not kidding. The girl's got a knack for collecting people." Glad slapped the side of her leg and yelled at Samson to quit digging in her garden.

"Dog." Gracie pointed and woofed.

Samson waddled over, wagging his stubby bulldog tail, his underbite resembling a goofy smile.

The glint in Red's gaze caught my attention. There was something deep inside her, and the curious part of me wanted to understand her confidence. I fingered the silver heart necklace my mother had given me as a child. I'd worn it nearly every day, taking it off only to shower and sleep.

"Do you ever feel like the past is closing in on you? Like if you're not careful, it'll grab you by the heels when you're least expecting it?" I steered the wagon to the creek. Not only had I collected stones from the rippling water, it was the place where Dad and I had some of our most meaningful conversations. Maria helped the girls from the wagon and played at the water's edge with them. Maggie and Glad watched on.

"I know what you mean. Time is weird like that." Red fiddled with her messy bun. Reaching down, she grazed the babbling water with her fingertips.

I knelt beside her. Bradley loved her. She was easy. She had a spark and a wicked grin that warned like a prowling tomcat. Picking up a pebble, I caressed its smooth surface, then flung it into the water.

"You gonna marry Matt someday?" Red asked.

I didn't say anything.

"Sorry. I shouldn't have overstepped that personal boundary." Red chose a gray stone with amber veins.

I lifted my chin to the sky, reminding myself

how minuscule I was in the realm of the universe. I leaned back on my heels until my bottom hit the ground. My arm brushed Red's as she sat beside me. She'd make a nice sister with or without Bradley.

"It's all right. I get that a lot." I held her stare. "I'm usually the one overstepping the boundary. You'll probably agree when you see the ideas I have for your wedding flowers and cake."

"We'll see." Red plucked a thick blade of grass.

"There's a baker in Bozeman who specializes in sugar flowers and romantic design. There's another one in Livingston who was on a baking show. Her painted buttercream cakes look like French art."

Red wrapped the grass around her finger.

"If you wrap that tight enough, your fingertip will turn purple," I said.

"Seriously. Matt's the father of your girls. He seems so perfect," she said under her breath.

"Nobody is perfect." I wrapped my arms around my knees and drew them to my chest. "Mostly me."

"Not sure what you mean." Red plucked more stones from the water.

"Especially me. There's always a crack, and my experience with cracks results in—brokenness. Seems like once I start to fix something, it only gets worse, and before I know it, the situation is beyond repair and I wish I wouldn't have touched it at all." I nibbled on the end of a piece of sweetgrass. "We're happy. That's the important thing."

"Marriage isn't for everyone." Red's piercing stare intensified. "But you don't strike me as the kind of woman who would scare easily. You ride like a bandit and are quick-witted. You certainly know your wedding cakes and can multitask. Or are those things cover-ups? What are you really afraid of?"

Red had turned the tables.

"You're good." I held her gaze. There was plenty to fear.

"Calling it like I see it," she said.

"I think I've finally met my match." A chill ran down my spine as her laugh drifted through the air between us. I leaned back on my elbows and stretched out my legs. "For me, mastering the parts of my life that come naturally doesn't dictate complacency. We're all a work in progress." I sucked in the sweet scent of sage. "I don't mean to be a downer. I don't think anything could ever come between you and Bradley."

"Nothing's for certain, but that's a chance I'm willing to take."

"Ouch," I whispered.

Red plucked a thick blade of grass and placed it between her thumbs. She lifted her hands to her lips. With one blow, the sharpest whistle I'd ever heard pierced the air. The girls looked over. Gracie smiled. I put my fingers in my mouth and blew my *it's time to come home* whistle. Gracie toddled over with Maggie and fell into my lap. Her giggle turned into a contagious belly laugh none of us could resist.

"Where did you learn how to do that?" I took the grass bouquet Gracie had picked.

"My uncle. He lived on a farm. I spent a lot of time there when I was a kid."

"Now we're getting somewhere. Serve it up, city girl. I'm listening." I paused. "That's if you're feeling like talking, because I'd love to hear about it." I wiggled my brows at her. "You always raise that eyebrow at people."

"It's a gift," Red answered.

"I think we have more in common than I think."

"My uncle's farm was charming in a run-down sort of way." Red closed her eyes, then slowly opened them. Her lips barely moved as she spoke. "It was safe there. There wasn't any drinking or men calling to collect debts or repossess anything.

When my parents lost custody, my uncle became my guardian."

Red had my attention, and I played with Gracie's blonde curls.

"Your family is everything mine wasn't," Red's voice trailed off.

"We're really a bunch of mavericks. Misfits with sass and heart. We all have baggage. It helps when you have someone who's willing to help carry the luggage."

Red chuckled. "I love Bradley to the moon and back. I'm really lucky."

"Bradley's lucky, too."

Her sincere tone confirmed my intuition regarding her relationship with my brother. Her confidence about love was unwavering. Her commitment tried and true. Red gazed at the mountain peaks in the distance. The petals of the flowers she'd put in her hair ruffled in the soft breeze. Red was beautiful inside and out, and I wanted some of what she had when it came to having faith in love.

"Bradley is pretty terrific, but don't tell him I said so. I'll never hear the end of it," I said.

Red pretended to lock her lips and throw away the key.

"Where is he, anyway?" I asked.

"You didn't cross paths when you came in?" Maggie lifted her chin to the sun.

Gracie patted my jean pocket, then dug her little fingers into it with a scrunched expression of determination.

"Just a second." I set her beside me in the grass. I shifted my weight to empty my pocket. "The girl knows I have sugar." I bit the sugar cube in half.

"Please," she said. "Tank, tank."

"That's *thank you* in Gracie language."

Lil caught us and made a beeline with Maggie's help.

"One nibble, then all gone." They opened their mouths like baby birds, waiting for the offering. I placed the sugar on their tongues. They held hands and savored the treat with a shared smile.

"Gone." Gracie stuck out her tongue.

Red handed me the miniature horseshoe that dropped from my pocket.

"Thanks. Wouldn't want to lose that." I put it away for safekeeping.

"If you're counting on that to lead the way, I think there's a more direct solution," Red said.

"Guess I'm a little superstitious."

"If you lose that, you'll still have those Montana stars you wish upon every night," Glad said.

"Everyone has power. The question you have to ask yourself is, do you want to ride or be ridden?" Red held my gaze.

"You're one tough cookie. I can see why you excel at being a business coach." I helped Gracie get her cowboy boots off, then handed her socks to Maria. "She loves to be barefoot."

"Tank. Tank." Gracie slid her feet against the grass, savoring each step.

"It's what I believe. The life lessons I find most valuable are the toughest and don't come from a textbook." Red lowered her gaze to the sun. Her freckles danced across her cheekbones.

Maggie respected Red, and it showed in her expression. Red was independent and had the will that made great leaders.

"Sorry. I have to learn not to do that," Red said. "Force of habit. I have to remind myself that not everyone is a client."

"Some people bank on winning the lottery. Others believe in fairies, and I believe in the stars and lucky horseshoes," I said. "The girls believe in sugar. One shouldn't leave home without it."

"Gracie is one smart cookie. Like her momma," Maggie said.

"This would be a beautiful place to get married. Candles. Lights that twinkle like the Montana stars. A traditional wedding cake. An elegant, silky dress. Cowboy boots. Music. Clinking champagne glasses. The scents of sage and leather. A bouquet of white." Red's faraway gaze smoldered.

"Cowboy boots, cologne, leather. What?" I was caught off guard with Red's daydreaming.

Maggie beamed.

"Sorry, I'm getting a bit caught up in the scenery. Your suggestion to get married here is appealing."

"I get it. I get carried away all the time. My grandparents had parties and dances in the barn back in the day." My spine tingled. "Maggie and Dad were married here."

"Yup. We were married right over there." Maggie pointed to the sprawling yard behind my house. "We had a gorgeous white tent. When dusk set in, it was even more picturesque with the sound of the river and the starry sky. It was like we were the only people on earth."

"Sounds grand." Red smiled.

"By the look on your face, I'm guessing you still remember," I said.

"Who could forget?" Maggie's voice cracked. "Bones got loose from the house. We're still not sure how. Are we, Chloe?"

"What? He was a smart dog." I shrugged.

"Not that smart," Maggie said.

"Who is Bones?" Red asked.

"A bulldog my mother gave me. She thought I needed a friend who could teach me a few lessons. He had a huge personality and could get into mischief with the best of them. Isn't that right, Chloe?"

"Dang," I said. "I can't believe you're still not over that. And I can't believe how you can still make me feel like I'm eight years old."

"It's a gift." Maggie tugged at the hem of her shirt. "One that I'm sure you will master as the girls get older."

Red threw her head back with a hearty laugh. "So what happened?"

"Remember those pink boots I wore with my party dress?" The breeze kissed my cheeks.

"Yes, I remember, but let's not skirt around Red's question." Maggie cleared her voice. "John and I had said our I dos, and all of a sudden, Bones came ripping across the pasture chasing the barn cats. Cocoa, Midnight, and Chloe's favorite, French Fry. Chloe named the cats back then."

"Still do, and proud of it," I added.

"The animals ran through the tent, under the cake table, and bam." Maggie smacked her hands together in a thunderous clap. "The cats parted ways, and Bones ran into the corner pole of the tent. He swayed, teetered backward, and fell into the leg of the table. If it wasn't for Chloe's granddad, we wouldn't have had cake. Bones knocked himself out cold. I thought he'd never come around, and if he did, he'd be even wackier than before he hit his head."

"Yeah, Grandpa swooped over and caught the cake. He was kind of like a superhero. If I remember right, we lost the plates and the candles though."

"Those were my *grandmother's plates*, thank you very much."

I rubbed my temple. "Yeah, somehow, I think I remember you telling me that. I *really* am sorry."

"I thought you didn't let Bones out of his crate," she said.

Maggie's hard stare was reminiscent of the days when I was a youngster causing my share of shenanigans. I searched her eyes for forgiveness.

"I think we've both known for a long time that it was my fault. In my defense, I was just a kid. I felt bad for Bones. He'd been in that crate a long time, and he was all alone."

Red sighed. "That's sweet."

"That's our Chloe. She's got the biggest heart of anyone I know. Still does. She can't turn down a horse without a home." Maggie patted my shoulder.

"It gets me into trouble. Pretty much every time. I did find a home for Sway and Domino though."

"But we're getting two new ones," Maggie said.

"What can I say? I'm a sucker for hope. The thought of something positive coming from the unfortunate makes me feel good. It's like rooting for the underdog." Red undid the bun at her nape. Her red locks flowed over her shoulders.

"Hope," Maggie uttered under her breath.

Maggie knew plenty about hope, and so did I.

"I know what you mean, but sometimes remaining hopeful is like treading water, and it's kind of scary when I can't touch bottom," Red said.

"Then you have to trust yourself not to sink," Glad replied.

I nibbled on my thumbnail, knowing her pointed reply was directed toward me.

CHAPTER 8

MARIA LOADED THE girls into their wagon. Lil couldn't keep her eyes open, and Gracie poked her to stay awake. I knew how she felt. Being in control meant keeping your eyes open at all costs. I kissed their muddy faces before Maria took them home for their much-needed naps. Maggie and Glad headed inside to start dinner.

Red and I met Matt and Bradley at the barn to saddle up a couple of easy-going horses for a ride along the river, then sent Red and Bradley on their way. With a two-way radio and the well-marked trail parallel to the river, Bradley's previous experience would lend nicely to a leisurely ride.

Tristan pulled into the drive with the two new horses. He parked the trailer near the empty pasture adjacent to the yard of my house. Sarah and Emma followed behind in Sarah's pickup truck. I waved from the front porch and answered Tristan's call.

"Hey, bosslady. They're here."

"Great. I appreciate you getting them settled. Is

something wrong though? I wasn't expecting Sarah." From a distance, I watched Emma get out of the truck. She stood at the fence with Tristan.

"Nope. Emma wanted to make sure they got here safely," Tristan replied.

"I'll be in the barn with Matt if you need me." I ended the call.

"Do you need me for something?" Matt went into the tack room.

I leaned against the doorjamb and crossed my arms over my chest. "Nope."

"You sure?" Matt stopped straightening the saddle blankets. "It's been my experience that your posture suggests otherwise."

After hemming and hawing, I figured I'd just speak up. "Red and Bradley are serious about getting married here when the renovation is done. I can't wait to taste wedding cakes with Red and decide on flowers. If they get married at Christmas, we could have sleigh rides. There's a lot to do before they go back to Boston."

"Good for them. Somebody should. Sounds like you've got it all planned." Matt went back to straightening the saddle blankets.

"What does that mean?"

"It means I can't find the blue plaid blanket that goes with my saddle. I had to use a different one, and well"—he scratched his temple—"it's just not the same without it."

I knew what he meant. I wished he hadn't brought up wanting to marry me at all. I walked over to the rack and pointed to the missing saddle blanket.

"It's right here on this bottom peg." I handed it to him. "Problem solved."

"I was serious when I said I want to marry you. I was hoping it would be sooner than later. I know you think marriage is a sure-fire way to end a relationship, but it doesn't have to be that way."

"Are you asking me right now to marry you?"

Matt took my hands in his. "No, Chloe. I promised you I'd have a ring and I'd get down on one knee. I want it to be romantic. So what if Bradley and Red want to get married here? Let them have their day. Just because you suggested it doesn't mean you have to plan it. You orchestrating it only makes me wonder why you're avoiding me."

"I want to throw a party."

"So throw one, and let them have their day their way." Matt laid the saddle blanket on the tack box.

I followed Matt, then tripped over him when he stopped short. He took me by the arm and brushed hair away from my cheeks. His dark stare made my belly flip and my blood run hot.

"I don't think I'll ever be ready." I swallowed the sticky hot knot at the back of my throat.

He mumbled something under his breath.

"What did you say?" I held his gaze.

"Nothing. I don't want to fight. I've got work to do. Branch has a few calves I'd like to take. You aren't the only one with a business venture in her hat."

"I know you're busy building a herd of your own." Irritation prickled. "Since when do you do business with Branch? All he's given Tristan are horses with attitudes."

Matt walked through the aisle at a quick clip.

"You're not going to say anything about Branch?" Talking to the back of his head wasn't an option.

"I don't want to fight." Matt disappeared into the office.

I stood in the doorway with my arms crossed over my chest. He rustled paper on the desk, slammed the desk drawer twice, then we stared at each other. Gypsy's neigh filled the silence between us.

"What's wrong with you? I thought women loved sensitive guys."

"I'm a little lost. You and me arguing about our differences won't solve anything. I'm not gonna start squealing like a momma sow being hog-tied at the county fair."

Matt left the barn without another word. He met my dad in the drive, and I watched them converse from the barn door. Whatever they were discussing involved quiet words. I turned on a heel and walked back into the barn to radio Tristan.

"How's it going?" I went to Gypsy's stall, and she poked her snout over the door.

"Good. The horses are settled. Sarah and I are just talking," Tristan replied.

"I'll be over in a bit." Gypsy tugged at the fabric of my shirt with her gentle nibble. Her attention made the uncertainty of the future slip away.

Sniffles came from the empty stall next to Gypsy. Emma sat in the corner, her back against the wall, her knees to her chest, her head down, her shoulders quivering.

I knocked on the timber beam to let her know I was there. I knew Lil and Gracie would have moments like this, too, and it broke my heart, because I'd had plenty of them growing up.

I sat next to her, knowing I didn't have words to fill the void she internalized. She wiped her eyes. I crossed my ankles and set my hands in my lap.

Sun drifted in through the window above our heads.

"Do you want to be alone?" I asked.

She shook her head. Her black bob skimmed her shoulders.

"I saw you helping your mom and Tristan with the horses. That was mighty nice of you."

Emma didn't respond.

"I did plenty of crying when I was your age."

Emma picked at the hem of her jeans.

"Your mom loves you very much. I'm pretty fond of you, too." The corner of my mouth lifted. "Trout, he's the guy with the white hair and moustache, he says words are overrated."

She scrunched up her face, found a tissue in her pocket, and wiped her nose.

"Smart girl. It's good to be prepared."

She tucked the tissue back into her pocket.

"Does your mom know you're in here?"

Emma shook her head.

"We should let her know you're okay."

She set her hand on my forearm when I started to get up. "Not yet."

"I like your pink nails. I bet my daughters will want to paint their nails someday. My mom will make sure they do. I'm not one to use polish." I showed her my nails. "I'm a biter."

"I'm a biter, too. The polish doesn't work like my mom thought it would."

"I guess we have something in common."

Emma cocked her head like a hunting retriever at the snap of a twig.

"I heard you talking to your mom last time you were here. I know you miss your dad."

Emma started to say something, then stopped.

"I like your boots. It's important for us cow-girls to like our boots. You never know when you're gonna have to run after a stray animal or child"—I smiled—"or have to walk miles because the truck broke down, or you just need to kick a bale of hay when things don't go right."

Emma stood. She walked to the other side of the stall and kicked the bale of hay.

"Sometimes, I have to kick it two or three times."

Emma kicked it again. She lowered her chin, pinched her eyes shut, opened them, clenched her fists, then kicked it one more time. She lost her balance when the toe of her boot lodged into the hay. I jumped up and caught her before she fell. She peered up at me from beneath her dark lashes.

"Friends don't let other friends fall."

Emma plopped down on the bale with a sigh and blew the hair away from her face.

"I'm not sure I've had a real friend before," she said.

"I know what that feels like, too. When I was little, my dad and I moved around a lot. When I moved here, the animals became my friends. I know you like the horses."

A slight smile worked its way into the seam of Emma's lips.

"Horses make the best friends. They're great listeners. Huckleberry could use a new friend. Want to meet her?" I held out my hand to Emma. "If not, it's okay. You can meet Huck another day." Emma squeezed my fingers as I drew my hand back. "Does that mean you want to meet her?"

She nodded.

We walked out of the barn. I pointed down the way, into the pasture where Trout was fishing at the pond. His fluid movements and line had peaceful rhythm. Huckleberry moseyed over when I whistled.

"My dad says I have too many horses. I can't stand it when a horse doesn't have a home." I took a piece of carrot from my pocket and fed it to Huck.

Emma climbed the fence rail to pet her.

"Huckleberry and I go way back. She's a sweet

one for sure." I took another chunk of carrot from my pocket and placed it in Emma's palm.

"My mom lets me feed the horses. When I'm not in school, I go with her when she makes house calls."

"That makes for a busy summer."

"I like going with her. I want to be a vet some-day, too." Emma fed Huck the treat. "Her lips tickle."

"Who knew a horse's lips could be so soft?" I played with Huck's mane. "Would you like to ride her? We'd have to ask your mom first."

Emma nodded. I called Tristan and cleared it with Sarah. After getting an okay, Emma and I went into the barn. She ran her fingers across the wooden stall doors as we made our way to the tack room.

"Maybe we should brush Huck first. I'll go get her. You wait here."

When I came back, Emma hadn't moved.

Emma stroked Huck's dark hide dotted with spots resembling deep purple huckleberries. Emma's rigid posture relaxed as she worked her way around sweet Huck.

"You're a natural. Do you have a horse?"

Emma shook her head.

"When you're here, you can dote on Huck and

ride her as long as your mom says it's okay." I picked Huck's frogs clean and saddled her up. "You ready?"

Emma nodded.

I handed her a helmet. "Safety first." With Emma's approval, I buckled it and tugged the chin strap snug.

Huck, Emma, and I made our way outside and into the pasture where she climbed the mounting block and waited for Huckleberry. Trout propped his rod against the tree trunk and came over to help.

"This is Trout. We've been friends since I was a kid."

"I'll hold Huck. You show your friend how to mount up," he said.

Emma put her foot in the stirrup and swung her leg over the back of the saddle like she'd been doing it her whole life.

"I like to ride." She lowered her chin.

Emma had her other foot set before I could check Huck's girth.

"I'll walk with you."

Trout went back to fishing while I led Huck around the field. Emma patted Huck's neck and fingered her mane. As we rounded the pond, Trout's lure got snagged in the low branch of the shade tree. He tugged and grunted, and I laughed at him.

"That's not something I see every day—or ever." I led Huck beneath the shade tree.

Emma peered through the branches and squinted into the sunlight. While I untangled the lure, Emma laid on Huckleberry like I did when I needed a hug. Sarah and Tristan stood at the fence. Emotion rose from the pit of my belly.

There had to be a way to make an animal therapy center happen. I'd make sacrifices to help children like Emma.

"We really should be going, Em. It's getting to be dinnertime. Can you tell Chloe thank you?" Sarah helped Emma from the saddle.

"Thank you." Emma took off her helmet and handed it to me. She hugged Huck and said goodbye.

"Emma's welcome to ride anytime. Huck's the perfect choice."

"Thank you," Sarah said, her expression almost apologetic.

Sarah and Emma made their way back to their truck. Emma waved from the open window as they drove past the pasture and out to the main road. Tristan took Huckleberry into the barn.

Trout cast his fishing line into the pond one last

time before packing up his gear.

"Looks like rain. We've been dodging showers all day." Studying the threatening clouds, Trout clicked his tongue against his teeth.

"Feels good out here." Cool raindrops dotted my arms, the wetness refreshing. I cupped my hands, letting the water pool in my palms. A fine mist filled the air.

"Sure does. Kind of steamy today."

The rain came down harder, and I let it wash over me like a cleansing blanket.

"We should get inside. You coming?" Wetness sat at the corners of Trout's moustache.

"In a minute. I'm thinking."

"That's what I'm afraid of."

"You sound like Matt," I said.

"Don't let it get the best of you." Trout paused. "Life's too short."

Rain dripped from the brim of my cowboy hat and onto my lip. I licked it away, thinking about Matt's kiss and his crazy idea to get hitched.

I picked up Trout's extra fishing pole and whipped it from ten to two. It cut the air in wicked slices.

"You haven't lost your touch, girl."

"Let's hope not," I said, meeting Trout's gaze.

"Something tells me we ain't talking 'bout fishing."

"We're not." Tugging on the line, I hooked a fish. "I know something about resistance, too. He's gonna have to work harder than that."

"Oh boy." Trout handed me the net.

"I don't need it. I'm gonna let him loose."

Trout hustled past me to the edge of the pond.

"Thought you were ready to go." I slipped on the grass, then grabbed his arm to keep from falling.

"Something tells me I should stay." Trout scooped the fish from the water.

"Take it easy." I cradled the fish in my hands, taking the hook from its mouth. The trout's spotted skin was vibrant even in the gray weather.

The rain came down harder. Thunder rumbled overhead.

"You ain't no different from the rest of us, kid. You've got something to do. It might not be easy, but letting it fester won't do any good. So quit dragging your spurs in the dirt and walk proud. You ain't never been shy about stirring the pot."

CHAPTER 9

AFTER REVIEWING THE estimates and multiple plans Mr. Featherstone sent over, Dad settled into the turquoise leather club chair in my office. I fiddled with the papers on my desk. Through the French doors behind him, Maggie and Glad danced with the girls while Maria picked up toys. Their animated waltzes and muffled giggles were a reminder of where I fit into the timeline in regard to history and the future of the McIntyre ranch.

"Did you notice that we're under budget, even with skylights? Mr. Featherstone and Mr. Cortright had some great ideas about design and materials without compromising structure. I've got a list of potential homes for some of the horses."

"I hear you loud and clear. There's still not enough for the therapy center you want to open. It's off the table, Chloe."

"I'll find a way," I said.

"I don't think you'll ever outgrow being a handful." Dad leaned forward on clasped hands.

"Can't blame a girl. The barn is an amazing

start. Thanks, Dad." I placed my hands atop his. No matter my age or stage of life, his touch was strong and comforting. I caressed his callused knuckles, knowing how much work I had before me to keep the homestead thriving.

"I never could say no to you, Chloe."

"You just did. Again." I fiddled with the silver horseshoe I used as a paperweight. "How much do you miss your parents?"

"More than anyone knows. When you lose someone, it leaves a hole."

"Grandpa was a cornerstone for me, but as time goes on, I'm learning Grandma was, too, even if we never met. I feel her. We are the women of Montana. And so are the two little ladies I'm raising."

"I know she sees you." He rubbed his chin, his eyes misty. "Your grandpa loved your grandma. She knew your granddaddy needed to be part of the land, and he was willing to follow her to the ends of the earth. What I wouldn't give to see them one more time."

I pointed to the living room. "Those doors are a looking glass. They're here. You know, that cigar box had letters in it. Apparently, Ida May told your dad they needed a ranch because you needed room to run and to have animals as companions. Lil and Gracie need the same thing."

"Chloe—"

"You know they do, too."

Maggie twirled Gracie around. She laughed so hard, she fell on her bottom and pulled Maggie down with her. Lil and Glad joined in the tickling.

"I'll let Matt know you're good with the plans. He should be home soon. Those new calves he's getting from Branch should put him in a good mood."

"I know he wants to marry you."

I held Dad's green gaze.

"By the look on your face, you're not ready to talk about it." He stood and opened the French doors.

"Pop-Pop!" Gracie ran to him.

He scooped her up and gave her a raspberry on her cheek. She laughed, then settled in his arms the way I used to. Maggie got to her feet. Lil climbed onto the sofa and snuggled next to Gladiola.

"Time for lunch." Maria stood in the archway wearing a plaid apron. "And I've got stew started in the crockpot."

Gracie sniffed the air and rubbed her belly. The girl loved food. With Glad's help, Lil got off the sofa and toddled over to Maria with open arms. Maria picked her up and toted her into the kitchen.

"I'll grab a sandwich before I head out." I tucked curly blonde hair behind Gracie's ear, then took her from my dad. "Let's go. It's naptime after lunch. Momma's got some wrangling to do."

"I hope you're referring to the cattle. The guys need your help," Dad said.

I ignored his comment.

Gracie fiddled with the bandanna I had tied around my head, then raspberried my cheek.

"Treat," Gracie said.

"Not until you eat your lunch, little girl."

Gracie blew kisses to my dad, Maggie, and Glad as they left the house through the front door. I took Gracie into the kitchen and got her settled into her highchair next to Lil.

"Why the long face? Did your meeting with your dad not go as expected?" Maria served the girls cubed peaches, cheese and crackers, and leftover chicken from last night's dinner.

"There's something I want to do, and my father's not on board."

"May I ask what?" Maria gave each girl a sippy cup of milk.

"I'd like to open an animal therapy center. We're missing out on a chance to help others. These horses have a bigger purpose." Moving forward with the center would help me process the questions I had in regard to my own purpose. Sure—there were plenty of books to read, but I wanted firsthand experience and validation.

"That's a great idea. Have you thought about writing a grant? There are alternative ways to fund projects if there's a money issue."

"I think it's more than money." I made myself a chicken sandwich, gobbled it down, kissed the girls, and headed out for the afternoon.

YESTERDAY'S RAIN HAD left us cooler air and slick muddy patches in some of the fields. Nearing the barn, Samson waddled out of the garden, his paws muddy from digging holes, no doubt.

"You are so naughty."

Samson wagged his stubby bulldog tail and puffed out his chest.

"Come on. I'll clean you up. Maggie and Glad are gonna know what you did."

We made our way into the barn. The wranglers were out mending fences and checking on cattle. I took a towel from the tack room and wrestled with Samson to wipe his paws.

"Ain't nothing gonna change the outcome regardless the resistance," Trout said. I got to my feet and turned around.

"I thought I was the only one here."

"I was in the shed organizing my fishing tackle. Saw you walk by." Trout tucked his hands in his pockets.

"Catch anything good?" I hung the dirty towel on a peg inside the tack room door.

"Guess that's all relative."

"Probably so." I opened the office door. Samson ran outside and rolled around trying to hanker some old itch.

"Those paws won't stay clean for long. Not to mention the rest of him."

"Probably not." I leaned against the doorjamb. "Not like you to follow me around without a reason. Go on, say it. You've been dishing it out since I was a kid."

"We all know you've got a way with animals— and people for that matter. But if you ain't careful, kid, you're gonna get a taste of your own medicine."

"You think I can't feel what's coming?"

"Nothing to be afraid of," Trout said with a grunt. He stepped outside and into the sunshine, lit a cigarette, and stared into the distance.

"Your cigarettes and cologne remind me of Grandpa."

"I ain't wearing cologne."

I lifted my chin to the breeze.

"Sometimes being your sounding board is like nails on a chalkboard. Makes me uncomfortable." Trout took a long drag from his cigarette, snubbed it out, and tucked the butt in his shirt pocket.

I pushed my shoulders back. "You still haven't told me why you're here."

"I don't like being in the middle. Compromise may just be a stepping stone for some, even if it isn't for you. Sooner or later, the ground becomes too uneven to see eye to eye."

"Not sure who we're talking about. And I didn't get to be the nails on a chalkboard without some help—had some fine mentors if I do say so myself."

"Not my place to say who's been airing their feelings."

"If I guess right, will you give me a sign?"

I said my father's name, then the wranglers. Trout didn't waver.

"Matt?" I lowered my chin at the twitch in his moustache. "Dang it. Cows or"—my belly rolled over with the words I was afraid to say—"you must know he wants to marry me."

Trout turned on a heel and walked away.

I went into the office and took the address book from the desk drawer. I'd ranked the horses according to disposition, noted their size, and what they were used for prior to coming here. We had plenty of great working horses, and I was prepared to let them go if it meant easing the budget with an agenda to open a therapy center. Antsier than ever, waiting for Matt to confront me about getting married or propose, I dove into my project, took the clipboard with the list of horses from the wall hook, and began making phone calls.

The thought of Matt on one knee, holding a ring, made me sweat. By the end of the first hour of telephone calls, I'd managed to find six of the fifty-two horses new homes. After the girls went to bed, I'd research grants. Emma wouldn't be the only one needing a therapy session with a four-legged friend.

CHAPTER 10

MARIA HAD GONE home for the day, and I was on mom duty. Lil and I gazed out the living room window. Red was stretched out in the thick grass fit for a fairy tale; the toes of her boots pointed toward the endless blue sky. With her chin to the sun, she propped herself up on bent elbows, her denim and leather impeccable. The wildflowers appeared to be bowing their heads in her direction. She resembled a model in one of Mom's fashion magazines.

I took Lil into the kitchen, buckled her in her high chair, snuck outside with the camera to snap a few frames, then came back in. I'd send Bradley the files later. Maggie had given me a camera and taught me about photography when I was pregnant with the twins and couldn't ride. It was easy to understand how Maggie's hobby turned a lifetime of chronicling her Montana life into a series of coffee table books. She had a knack for storytelling without the written word.

"What are we going to do while your sister

finishes her nap?" I tickled Lil's chin. "Maggie and Glad are in cahoots about something at the main house. They think I don't know, but I do." Lil slapped her high chair tray, her brown gaze as soulful as her daddy's. I picked her up, and we peered out the kitchen window at Red.

"That girl's got a lot on her mind. She didn't even realize I was out there."

Lil sputtered in my ear and weighed down my hip. Truth be told, I wasn't so sure I wanted her to speak in sentences. The phone rang, and I answered it.

"Hi, Maggie. Are you and Glad done conspiring?"

"Yep," she answered. "Are the girls up from their naps?"

"Just Lil."

"Call me when they're both up. The wagon and horses are ready to go. We're going for a ride."

"Are Dad and Bradley joining us?"

"Nope, just us girls."

"Sounds fun. What about dinner? Maria's got dinner in the crockpot."

"Got it covered. Put it in the fridge for tomorrow."

Cries from upstairs filled the house. "Gracie's up."

"You're not kidding. Boy, is she loud. We'll pick you up." Maggie ended the call.

"Let's get your sister," I said to Lil.

The back door shut, and Red came in. "I'll take Lil," she said.

"Gladly." Lil's face soured, and I was sure she understood my sarcasm.

"Do you mind changing her before Maggie and Glad get here? They've got something planned." Red couldn't hide her wry smile. "Obviously, you already know," I said.

"Yes, I do. It'll be fun. Can't let Bradley leave without a proper farewell."

"Where's he going?"

"Boston. Something's popped up at the firm, and he can't handle it from here. He's flying out tomorrow, but I'm staying. I haven't had a vacation in forever. We're having a weenie roast by the river."

"Yay, Auntie Red is staying." Lil covered her ears as Gracie's cry grew louder. "I know. Someone isn't happy."

I hustled upstairs. At the top of the landing, I stopped to look at a black-and-white photo of Ida May that hung on the wall. She sat in Grandpa's vintage pickup, arms propped on the open window sill. The photo was one of my favorites. The lace curtains at the end of the hallway billowed, and the breeze swaddled me in what I believed to be her spirit.

"Coming, Gracie," I called, thinking my voice would calm her. When I opened the door, my heart raced. Gracie sat on the floor with tears in her eyes.

"Are you okay, baby girl? Climbing out of your crib isn't such a great idea." Scooping her up, I held her close. "I know, hurting your pride stings more than the fall sometimes."

"You're telling me," Red said.

I inspected Gracie for bumps and bruises but found nothing. I rocked her until she stopped whimpering. "Come on, you two. We're going out to dinner. But first, clean undies and clean shirts. I can't wait for these two to be potty trained." Another note to self—I'd use the money spent on diapers and pullups for the therapy center. That small fortune would be helpful.

"I think Lil could use a sweater," Red said, touching my daughter's button nose. "You two are a lot of work."

"Don't I know it. Thank goodness for Maria, Maggie, and Glad. What would I do without them?"

"I don't know." Glad peeked into the bedroom. "What's going on in here? I could hear Gracie's howl down the road."

I raised an eyebrow in Glad's direction. "No, you didn't."

"Okay, I didn't, but it sure wasn't the welcome I'd intended when I came to get you girls." Glad entertained Lil with a fuzzy lamb while Red found Lil's horsey cardigan.

"Good grief, is Gracie okay?" Maggie poked her head into the girls' bedroom.

"I think she's fine. She climbed out of her crib."

Maggie shook her finger at Gracie. "She's gonna be in a big girl bed before you know it."

"Then you'll need to make sure the doors are locked so she can't leave the house." Glad made her mother-knows-best face.

"Yeah, yeah. I know where you're going with this. Apples don't fall far from the tree. We've already established that." I waved my hands around in circles after handing Gracie to Maggie. I balled up Gracie's dirty shirt and tossed it into the hamper. "She shoots, she scores."

"Taking after your momma is going to leave you with a few bumps and bruises," Maggie said.

"You're going to get them anyway—with or without me," I whispered in my daughter's ear.

Red found a red paisley bandanna in the plastic bin of hair accessories on the shelf and tied it around Lil's neck. Lil tugged at the fabric, so I took the bandanna from my head, rolled it up, and did the same.

"Now we're twins." I showed her in the mirror. "Very chic. My mother would approve," I said.

Gracie whimpered and reached for her sister's scarf.

"You can have one, too." Red found a flowered bandanna my mom had made for them. After tying it around Gracie's neck, Red picked her up and showed her in the mirror. Gracie clapped.

"Now that everyone's all duded up, it's time for country diner dinner," Maggie said with a mischievous grin.

"We haven't had one of those in a long time." I gave her a thumbs-up.

"Country diner dinner?" Red questioned.

"Diner dinners are our way of making ourselves feel better. Can't go wrong with grilled hot dogs, hamburgers, fries, and milkshakes after a *poopy* day. But there's a riff tonight since we're eating around the bonfire." Maggie sniffed Lil. "Pun intended. And by the smell of things, you smell lovely."

I scooted out of the room and down the hallway, then returned with scarves for Maggie. Glad, and Red. "Now we're ready. Red, you might want a jacket." I motioned for everyone to follow me.

"These scarves are beautiful." Red admired the fabric printed with Montana wildflowers and embroidery.

"My mom designed them."

"With your help," Glad added. "You've got many hidden talents, Chloe."

"You're sweet. C'mon now." Uncomfortable with the praise, I hurried them along. "Is Bradley upset about leaving early?" I put Lil down at the bottom of the steps and threw on Matt's denim jacket from the hall closet. The scent of his aftershave washed over me. Nothing beat being wrapped in the lingering aroma of *my* cowboy.

"He's disappointed," Red said.

We all made our way into the kitchen, where I packed a tote for the girls. Outside, I got into the driver's seat of the wagon.

"You drive," Glad said to Maggie.

"Why?" I placed the tote behind me.

"I like it better when Maggie drives."

"I'm a stellar driver." I shrugged off Glad's uncertain expression.

"One of these days, you're gonna realize being

a passenger can offer a sense of peace. And if you're not gonna let Maggie drive, I'm sitting up front." Glad maneuvered her way next to me. I held out my hand to steady her; she waved me away. "I got it. I got it," she grumbled.

"You're in a mood."

Glad leaned over. "Worked like a charm. I get to be baby-free and help steer this thing."

"Um, I'm not so sure that's a great idea." I held the reins tighter.

"Killjoy. At least teach me how it works. If Granny on *The Beverly Hillbillies* can have a shotgun, I can drive a wagon. What's the big deal? You're sitting right here, and I'm not getting any younger."

"Fine, I'll teach you."

"Oh boy," Maggie said. "We'll find my mother out here on a runaway wagon, and the guys will have to retrieve her. It'll be like having a fool-headed teenager again."

"This is how you take the brake off." I gestured to my foot not even sure, Glad had enough strength to release the metal petal. "Hold the reins like this." I clicked my teeth and gave the horse a sharp "ya!" Their ears perked up, and they trotted at an easy gait.

"I want to learn, too," Red said.

"We'll be a band of runaway women together. Won't that be exciting! Ya!" Glad shouted before steadying herself.

Heavy hooves against the ground washed out Gracie and Lil's giggles. My Montana twins loved a bumpy ride. Probably a good thing, since I was their momma.

The firepit was about ten minutes away by wagon. We rode through the pine grove, past Trout's cabin, and into a wooded area, where we stopped near the riverbank. Paper lanterns hung from low-lying branches. Sapphire-blue birthday balloons were strung on twine and secured to the trees, defining the getaway we'd cleared for just such a day. Trout and Tupelo Honey waited for us.

"Whoa." My voice was deep, like one of the guys. Glad stared at me with bright eyes.

"If you're not careful, you'll grow scruff like all the cowboys around here. Except for Tristan. He's the only clean-shaven one."

"Hope not." I set the brake, taking in the sight.

"Hey, I didn't get to drive." Glad pouted.

"Maybe on the way back," I told her.

"We'll see," Maggie said from behind us, shaking her head.

A storm crossed Glad's gaze. She was bound to

get her way sooner than later. I climbed down from the driver's seat, then helped Glad to solid ground.

"Looks like a party." I helped Gracie down the steps at the rear of the wagon.

"It is," Maggie said. "I didn't have those kidney stones without reason. Had to get Bradley here so we could celebrate his birthday and yours."

Gracie's eyes sparkled in the late-day sun. The firepit glowed. Crackles and pops sent fleeting sparks into the air. With everything going on, celebrating birthdays hadn't crossed my mind.

"Happy birthday, kid." Trout winked.

"Thanks, cowboy. I'll get my hug later. I know how you feel about having an audience. Where are the guys?"

"Bradley wanted to ride. They should be here soon. They took the long route. In the meantime, we can get the vittles set up on the table." Glad placed a rock on top of the napkins, then opened a cooler.

"Vittles," Maggie repeated. "She's *definitely* been watching television reruns."

"Ain't nothing wrong with a classic." Trout took the bowl of bean salad from Glad and set it on the table.

"As long as you don't beg for a cement pond,

it's all good." Maggie gave her mom a peck on the cheek.

"You gonna kiss me when you're all grown up, Lil?" Lil pressed her lips to my chin. "That's my girl." Gracie mimicked her sister's action and kissed Red, then played with her long tresses.

"Watch her. She might pull," Maggie said.

Faint sounds of banter drifted through the trees. Dad led the way. He was perched tall in the saddle. "Look, Pop-Pop is riding *my* Gypsy."

"He knew if she didn't get her exercise, she'd be a handful tomorrow," Maggie said.

"That's my girl. She doesn't like being cooped up."

"Kind of like someone else we know." Glad reached into a canning jar. "Can't beat these homemade pickles." She nibbled with puckered lips.

Bradley rode behind on Casanova, one of Tristan's wild ones gone soft, maneuvering through the trees.

"Looking good, big brother."

"Great, can I ride him? I'd love to run him." The thought gave me goose bumps. Gypsy whinnied and threw her head back.

Tristan tipped his hat and tied his horse to the hitching post. "All you have to do is ask."

"You two might want to discuss that out of earshot." Dad tied Gypsy to the hitching post. "This one's mighty sensitive. She's not a fan of you working in the office."

"Neither am I. We could've used your help today. The calves were a handful," Matt said.

Lil's smile grew wide like the open valley. Matt and I believed my grandparents had a hand in bringing the girls to us, and the breeze tickling my skin validated it.

"I love you, girl." I touched Gypsy's starred forehead.

"Love you, Momma." Lil played with my scarf.

"Did you hear that?" I glanced around.

Maggie clapped.

"Feels good, doesn't it?" Glad nibbled on a strawberry. "Now, that's a birthday present!"

Red strolled over with Gracie.

"Hey, Gracie girl. How about you? I love you." A silly glint sparkled in her green eyes. She smiled, then pressed her lips to my cheek. A lather of bubbles coated my skin. Wincing, I wiped away the slobber and met my father's gaze. "Thanks for teaching her how to give raspberries."

"Happy birthday, sweetheart." Dad chuckled.

"That's *your* daughter." Matt laughed, then secured Trigger to the hitching post. "Come here,

Gracie. Papa wants a kiss, too." She wrapped her arms around Matt's neck. She had eyes only for her daddy. Gracie nuzzled close, then kissed him on the cheek.

"That's *my* girl. Now, if only we could get your momma to settle in, we'd be all set."

CHAPTER 11

MAGGIE, RED, AND Glad drove Bradley to the Bozeman airport after breakfast. For the rest of us, it was business as usual. Matt and the wranglers had headed out to check on the cattle. I stayed behind to work with my dad.

We inspected the open space inside the old barn. Featherstone's crew had removed all the rotted wood, taken out one of the stall walls, and stacked the salvaged wood outside. Dad and I discussed the original reconfigured floor plan and agreed it made sense. The two extra stalls, tack room, and small bathroom worked for us. Dad checked the time.

"Maggie and Red should be back from the airport soon." I paced in the aisle.

"Maggie's bummed Bradley had to leave early." Dad ran his hand over a horizontal wooden dowel that had held horseshoes.

"Something you'll never have to worry about, because I'm staying forever. Lucky you."

Dad knocked his hat back. "Lucky me."

"It'll be great having two bathrooms out here." I stepped over the tape marking the welcome addition. "Can't wait to see it all done. Thanks to Mom, I found the perfect sink to mount in the aisle. It looks like a trough and stands on iron legs. Totally barn worthy. The woman's got an imagination."

"Don't we all know it." Dad leaned against the doorjamb. "You okay with Bradley and Red getting married here? Seems like you're in high gear."

"Helping Red with the wedding is a good idea. Besides, I suggested it. With another project on my plate—"

Dad finished my sentence.

"You won't have time to think about Matt's proposal?" He sighed. "Chloe, not everyone wants to be one of your projects. Maybe it'd be better if you focused on yourself. When Matt accepted the co-CEO position, he told me. The boy wants a wedding. He wants his girls to know he loves their momma in a traditional way. He asked for my approval, and I gave it to him."

"This is something he and I should work out." Lola ran into the barn, and Samson waddled behind. Lola barked at me, then jumped into my arms. "Thank goodness for the calvary."

"I wanted you to know. I told you a long time ago I wouldn't meddle in your relationship, and I won't start now. I wanted you to know he and I spoke." Dad crossed his arms over his chest. "*Now* you can change the subject. This barn brings back good memories."

I set Lola down, patted Dad's shoulder, and strolled outside. Lola and Samson woofed and followed on my heels.

"I don't have any treats." I shooed them away. Lola scooted beneath the timber fencing and into the pasture. Samson trotted ahead and back into Maggie's garden.

The stories Red told about her uncle's farm stuck with me. It had been her safe place. Her uncle had become her constant, helped shape her career. Emma obviously liked it here, and this ranch seemed to be a safe place for her, too.

A pickup hauling a gooseneck horse trailer came down the drive. I checked my phone. Mr. Phillips was right on time. Tristan greeted him at the barn as I made my way over.

"What's this about?" Dad asked.

"Mr. Phillips lives ten miles east of Livingston. He's in the market for horses."

"Hey there. Thanks for coming out today." I shook his hand and introduced my dad. "Thanks for giving them a good home."

As Tristan and Mr. Phillips loaded the horses, I leaned into Dad. "Mr. Phillips bought six; the two new pintos are gone. Figured it would be a good idea not to get attached. I also donated three to a children's program associated with Glad's women's club. That makes eleven. All going to excellent homes."

"No, Chloe. That's great you're doing your part to free up the budget, but it won't change my mind about housing a therapy center."

"I didn't ask."

"It's not in the cards." He rubbed his chin.

"I've mentioned it to Matt."

"I know," Dad mumbled.

"And—"

"And, it's not in the cards."

"I'm gonna miss those horses. Saying goodbye is hard," I said.

"I know, sweetheart. Fewer horses means you can focus on the cattle more. You haven't been in the field much lately. The wranglers need you."

"They'll be fine."

Mr. Phillips left a dusty trail behind him. Tristan waved and disappeared into the barn.

"Eleven horses, Dad. I have a lead on alternative funding, and Matt has experience writing grants."

"My wallet appreciates your hard work, but no. Be the foreman you signed on to be." He tugged at the brim of his hat, got into his pickup, and rolled down the window. "Tell Maggie I'll be back in an hour or so. And because I'm your father—don't put yourself at the bottom of the to-do list."

The tug in my heart was very real. There were children out there who needed a place to go and animals to love. All roads led home, and if I could be part of the journey for someone who needed a helping hand, I wanted to be there for them.

Matt rode in on Trigger, dismounted, and tied his best horse to the hitching post.

"What's with the long face, Momma?"

"I've rehomed eleven horses and Dad still says no to a therapy center."

Matt took off his leather gloves and slapped them against his thigh.

"I was thinking you could use your excellent business skills to help me write a grant for funding."

"There are strings attached to the money, Chloe. It's not like you get it and you're free and clear."

"So let's find the right strings."

"It's not that easy."

"Sounds like you and my dad are on the same side of the fence."

"It's not about taking sides."

Maggie and Red came up the drive and headed toward the main house. Matt wrapped his arm around my shoulders and gave me a squeeze.

I'D PUT THE girls to bed, taken a long hot soak, and in that quiet time had an epiphany or two, or so I thought. Wrapped in my cotton robe, I sat on the bed and opened the cigar box filled with memories my grandparents kept. I took the silver horseshoe from the box and leafed through the letters, trying to decide which one to read next. I chose a yellowed envelope addressed to Ida May.

Matt sat on the edge of the bed. His whiskers tickled my skin as I read the letter to him.

Dear Ida May,

Where are you going to house the cattle? Have you told Winston you bought them yet? I'm sorry buying Bundt's ranch didn't work out. The Lord works in mysterious ways. Determination will get you through the tough times. Your love for the land and cattle will lead you home. Keep the faith as I do with my Jackson. He's spent the money you paid him for the White Park and can't refund your payment. I'm sorry I can't be more help. Praying.

Margaret.

"Apparently, my grandmother had a hand in getting Grandpa's cattle. Look—Grandma wrote on the back." I flipped the letter over.

"Dear Margaret,

I appreciate your friendship and concern. I shouldn't have spent the money without telling Winston. I thought the ranch was a done deal. The cattle will be a greater surprise than expected. I wonder if the owner of the house we rent allows pets.

Ida May

p.s. Guess there's no sense in passing notes in church anymore. Pretty soon, Winston will know about the cattle."

I read the last exchange.

I.M.

Although you have a great sense of humor, I'm not sure you can get away with having them as pets. Keep me posted. John says they have to go soon.

p.s. Passing notes in church makes me feel like a schoolgirl."

I folded the letter and tucked it back in the envelope.

"Things do have a way of working out. Why don't you put those old letters away?"

"I'm glad whatever ranch they lost happened, because the 617 was meant to be." I shivered as Matt brushed the hair away from my neck. "I wonder how upset Grandpa was with Ida May for buying cattle."

"Obviously, they worked through the issue. That's what marriage is all about, and the girls are asleep. How about some alone time?" The corner of his lip curled.

"Can you imagine Winston kissing my grandmother?"

"Not if she was as stubborn as you."

"You're funny." I faced him.

"Chloe McIntyre." He put the letter in the cigar box. "You're being kind of bossy." He rubbed my bottom lip with his thumb.

"Do you think I take on projects to avoid my feelings and conflict?"

"I do. I was hoping your effort to help Red plan a wedding was your way of dipping a toe in the marriage pond."

"You're certainly frank."

He leaned against the heavy headboard with a grunt. "I'm beginning to think there's no good time to discuss anything."

I shut the cigar box and set it on the nightstand.

"Let's not ruin tonight." Matt's gaze flickered.

He unbuttoned my plaid shirt and pushed it away from my shoulders. He traced my collarbone, letting his fingers wander down to my belly.

"You wear my shirts well," he whispered.

"I like how they smell." Matt's lips warmed my skin.

"I think your wish is going to come true, Momma."

"Not sure what wish you're referring to."

"You usually get what you want. You're quite the puppet master."

"A puppet master. *Really?*" I laid back against the pillows. His sultry expression ignited a tingle beneath my skin. "You're one fine cowboy, Matt Cooper." *That* truth was easy to articulate. I pulled him close. Every cell of my being quivered. I hadn't planned on wavering feelings.

"That's more like it."

"I just want everything to be perfect." I rumpled the sheet in my fist.

"Perfect isn't possible. Sometimes waiting for

perfect is an excuse for putting something off you really don't want in the long run."

My heart raced as I took in his words, his loving touch, and attentive nature. Matt took my hands in his and traced the lines in my palms.

I could barely speak. "How do you feel about a prenup? Should we protect ourselves?"

Matt smoothed the hair away from my cheeks. His chest rose and fell in the quiet. I waited for a response.

"That's charming, Chloe. Your need to control things is taking the fun out of it. I should've just gotten down on one knee and proposed."

I dropped my chin, releasing the tension in my shoulders. He lifted my gaze and stroked my cheek.

"Go to sleep, Chloe. You've been in that office of yours a lot lately when you should be in bed. You need your sleep more than you need an animal therapy center. Bradley and Red will understand, probably appreciate the step back. I know I will. The girls deserve a rested momma, and I need the foreman of this ranch to get back to business. I need you to be you."

I rested my head on his chest until he fell asleep, then kissed him before getting out of bed. There was a grant to write and wedding plans to organize.

CHAPTER 12

THE SUNNY HAZE pushed its way through the valley, bringing a new day. I sipped my coffee while taking in the Montana landscape from my office. Notes pertaining to grants along with a list of potential benefactors littered my desk. Getting my rear end in the saddle was a must this morning. I wasn't up for a lecture about shrugging off my foreman duties.

I'd stayed up late and still found it difficult to sleep. Matt was on my mind twenty-four seven. There had to be a way for us to come to an agreement about our relationship without compromising it or worse.

Maria arrived early and was curled up on the sofa with the baby monitor, something she normally didn't do. I stood in the living room doorway, nibbling my nails.

"Are you okay?" I asked.

"I stayed up reading last night until two for the online education class I'm taking. My girlfriend, Ally, said the summer classes covered the same amount of material as a regular semester. She was right." Maria sat up and propped her feet on the ottoman.

"Did you get your reading done?" I sat next to her.

"Yes. Now to finish the project. We have to draw and label a floor plan for a kindergarten classroom. The prof gave us a $700 budget for teaching tools and toys. We have to create a purchase order with pictures and prices. Seven hundred dollars doesn't go far. I'm learning teachers in the field spend a lot of their own money on supplies." She reached into her backpack for the *Teacher Time* catalog, sticky notes marking the pages with potential items.

"When the girls rest today, you rest. If the chores don't get finished, it won't be the end of the world. At what point in your coursework will you work with children? Do you keep in touch with the director of the daycare you worked at before coming here?"

"My senior year, and yes, I still talk to her. I even babysit Jack sometimes."

"I remember him. He wasn't happy you came to work for us." I took the throw from the back of the sofa and draped it over Maria. "The girls slept through the night. Hopefully, they'll sleep a bit longer for you."

MATT RODE AHEAD with Dad, and I trailed behind combing the hillside for stray horses. The two seemed more inseparable with each passing day. Matt's serious nature and integrity bred loyalty. He was the perfect co-CEO. His allegiance to my dad and business came first. Persuading either one of them seemed impossible.

Boomerang, Tristan's toughest acquisition, peeked out from behind a shaggy pine. "I see you, girl." I ducked beneath the low-lying branches as Gypsy maneuvered through the dense grove. Boomerang shook her head at us. "Come on, girl. It's time to run."

Her mysterious soul shone through her icy blue gaze. "It's just like you to give me a hard time." Clicking my tongue at her, I prodded her to get going. "Dang, you're as hardheaded as Tristan."

"Hey, I heard that." Tristan's voice drifted through the thick air.

"This horse of yours won't budge. I can barely see you through the fog."

"You're not kidding." Tristan emerged, his wide-brimmed hat snug against his brow, his temperament as light as daybreak. Something that didn't come easy for him.

He put his fingers between his teeth and whistled. "Let's go, girl."

Boomerang thrashed her head back and forth.

"When this fog lifts, I bet the sky will open up with a sea of blue." Gypsy picked her path through the exposed tree roots. "It's gonna be a nice day. I can feel it in my bones."

"What day in Montana isn't nice?" Tristan asked.

He swatted Boomerang on her hindquarters. She pawed at the ground.

Gypsy did a quick sidestep. "Wonder what's got her in a snit?"

"Hope it doesn't snarl and have big teeth." Tristan scanned what little area was visible.

The white blanket of mist surrounding us was no barrier to nature.

"I've got my bear spray."

"Don't go getting all nervous on me, bosslady. Not quite your style. It's bad enough Boomerang won't budge. What's the matter, girl?" he asked as if she could answer. She sniffed the ground.

Putting wildcat or bear out of my mind, I dismounted Gypsy, stepped closer to the antsy horse, and inspected the base of the tree she hugged.

Something poked through the soil.

"What are you doing?" Tristan leaned over to see what I tugged at.

"There's something here, but I can't quite see what it is." Boomerang's breath warmed my neck. I lost my balance when she nudged me from behind. My hat came loose, and my rear end hit the ground. Brushing away the dirt, I yanked at the metal lodged in the soil. "This is really stuck."

"Dang, girl. You're gonna hurt yourself."

Tristan climbed down from Hitchcock and crouched beside me. I dug at the ground with a sharp stone, and he wiggled the metal object free, knocking me off my feet again, then grabbed my hand to help me up.

"It's just an old horseshoe," he said.

"This is no Montana sapphire, but I'll take it." I wiped it clean with my bandanna, then inspected it. I wanted to believe it was a Montana treasure special enough to get my therapy center.

My radio crackled with Matt's voice. Boomerang whinnied, then trotted off. Her black hind end disappeared into the fog. Tristan cupped his hands for me to use as a step to mount Gypsy, who appeared twice as tall on the incline.

"You must think I'm a fool." I hoisted myself up.

"No, I think you're a dreamer. I bet money

you'll be wishing upon that old thing before we get home."

Gypsy's ears went back with a snort. Her attention focused on the pasture in the distance. Boomerang had a head start, and Gypsy wanted to take the lead as much as I did.

"My wife, Viv, was a dreamer, too. I kind of like that in a woman." Tristan clicked his tongue and winked.

"News flash, we've all got dreams and destinations." I tucked the horseshoe in the pocket of my jacket.

"Yes, we do, bosslady." Tristan prodded Hitch to race ahead.

Gypsy and I followed. "Hey!" I called to him as Gypsy closed the gap between us. "Hey!"

"Hey, what?" he replied.

I ignored my thought of avoiding the subject of Tristan's deceased wife. "Vivian was a dreamer?" Gypsy pulled at the reins, ready to release her morning energy.

"Biggest dreamer I ever knew." Tristan lowered his chin as Hitch slowed to a lazy gait.

The horseshoe in my pocket bumped against my ribs. Knots tightened in my belly. By the expression on Tristan's face, I hadn't pressed my luck.

"You're a fool-headed woman, Chloe McIntyre." Tristan straightened his posture.

The chilly air bit my nose.

Tristan seemed different today. He'd said Vivian's name on purpose. But Matt and Dad were waiting for us in the field with the herd, eleven shy of not enough in my opinion but eleven closer to looser purse strings.

"You ready, cowboy?"

"Not today. That blue sky you're counting on won't be here for a bit. It's starting to rain, and it's getting slick. You'd be smart to mind your way," Tristan called.

I whistled, crouched low in the saddle, and gave Gypsy a quick kick. "Ya!" I slapped the reins from side to side.

Before I knew it, wild beauty surrounded me, flailing manes and the sound of unharnessed temptation. Gypsy nosed out the other horses. The thunder of pounding hooves drove her harder. Not willing to lose the lead, I hunkered down and focused on the corral in the distance.

Gypsy's smooth gait took me home.

We crossed the bridge. Gypsy lost her balance with the surface change beneath her feet. I held tight as she slid through the slippery mud. We went down with an echoing thud.

Matt's voice boomed over the fading thunder.

Face down in the grass, I turned my head. Gypsy's dark eyes pleaded for help.

"Gypsy!" I reached for her, ignoring the thorny thistle against my cheek.

"Chloe!" Matt dismounted before Trigger came to a screeching halt.

I grabbed my side.

"Chloe!" Dad yelled.

A strange haze numbed my senses, and my eyelids drifted shut. Matt cradled my head in his lap.

"Chloe, can you hear me?"

No words came. I'd never fallen like this before, and I thought I never would. Opening my eyes took monumental effort. Someone stroked my limbs.

"Dad," I whispered. "Is Gypsy okay? Where's Gypsy? Did she get up?"

"Lie still," Dad's soft words didn't hide concern. What part of me was hanging by a thread? The ground shook with the sound of a mounting stride.

"It's Tristan," Matt said.

I peeked through my lashes; three of the strongest men I knew watched over me. "Where's my girl?"

"She's here," Dad said.

"Is she still down?" No one answered me. I swallowed my emotion, the taste of losing Gypsy more bitter than a Montana winter. I reached for the hand patting my jacket. Something in my side stabbed like a dagger.

"What's she got in here?" Matt's voice tickled my ear. "What's she doing with this horseshoe?"

"She found it on the hillside," Tristan said.

"I'm sorry. I tried to hang on." Matt caressed my forehead. His touch was everything, period. I didn't want him to leave my side.

"Does your head hurt?" Dad asked. "I don't feel any bumps. There's no blood."

"I don't think my head hit the ground. Where's Gypsy?"

"She's here." Matt patted my hand.

Wetness seeped from the corners of my eyes.

"Can you get up?" Matt stroked my cheek.

"I think so. Just give me a minute." I bent my knees, sat up, and rubbed my head.

I caught sight of my Gypsy lying on the ground next to my hat. Trout stroked her twitching muscles. I prayed she'd settle down and not hurt herself more. Matt scooped me up and carried me to the main house.

MATT SET ME on the sofa and placed a pillow behind my head. Maggie handed Dad his medical bag. Dad examined my eyes. Concern lined his expression.

"Let me see your ribs," Dad said.

"I'm fine. Gypsy needs me." His grip tightened on my arm, and he shushed me as I tried to sit up. "Fine, I'll let you look, but I don't think I broke anything."

"Good, because if you don't let me check you thoroughly, we're going to the hospital. Your choice."

"Living with a doctor has its advantages," Maggie said.

"What's all the fuss?" Glad's shrill tone sounded panicked.

"Gypsy and I went down." Dad continued to hover over me. "It's not like Gypsy rolled on me or my feet got stuck in the stirrups. People fall off horses all the time."

"Let your dad check you out," Glad said. "I'm not asking. I'm telling." Her voice trembled.

I'd never seen her this upset. She rested her hand on my shoulder.

"It's just that—" Dad stuck a tongue depressor in my mouth.

"I'll take this out of your mouth if you promise to stay quiet," he said. "You've still got all your teeth.”

I did my best to hide the ache in my bones. Giving in, I sighed. “I don’t want an audience.”

“You don’t have to have one.” Glad wrung her hands, then left.

“We’ll give you some privacy.” Maggie paused. “John, let me know and I’ll make the call.”

“I’ve examined enough bodies in my lifetime. Please, cooperate?”

Staring up at him, I unbuttoned my shirt. He took my boots and socks off, feeling my ankles and legs.

“Can you stand?”

“I’m a little shaky,” I said.

He helped me to my feet, raised my tank, and tucked it under the band of my bra. He pressed here and there, then stood behind me. I shut my eyes. His fingers wandered across my shoulder blades. He traced the horseshoe tattoo on my left shoulder. I’d gotten it in college, wanting the exact ink my dad had.

Dad examined my extremities not once but twice, and then a third time. Matt paced.

“You need X-rays.”

“I don’t want—” I stopped myself from the usual banter. “Okay. I’ll do whatever you think is best.”

"I'll call Doc Porter. He's got the equipment in that new office of his. We'll go into Bozeman if he says so."

I tucked in my tank. Matt helped me with my shirt, socks, and boots.

"Chloe—" His breathy tone faded.

"I'll be fine," I said. "Please, tell me what's going on with Gypsy." I raised my voice. "Somebody just tell me."

"Trout's looking her over," Matt said.

My bottom lip quivered. "I'll see Doc Porter, but I want to see my horse first. Tell Maria where we're headed and that I'll call her if I have to go to the hospital." Wincing, I took the bandanna that once belonged to my grandmother from my rear pocket, traced her initials, then asked Matt to help me tie it around my head. I hobbled from the room, forcing one foot in front of the other.

Maggie waited in the foyer. She took my face in her hands. "Trout called. Gypsy's not in good shape. I'm sorry, Chloe." She paused. "He thought you'd want the truth." Her tone was soft as angel wings.

"He's right," I said. Matt and Maggie tucked a hand beneath each arm to steady me. "Waking up tomorrow is gonna hurt."

Outside, Maria pulled the girls in the wagon.

Red's expression as she walked alongside reciting nursery rhymes reminded me of literature class. She wore a shade of melancholy I'd only read about. All she needed was a flowing gown and silken slippers.

"Momma," Lil cooed.

"Hi, baby girls. You're very fashionable in those sweaters and beanies." I patted Lil's head, then kissed her hand. "Maria must've given you a bath. You smell like lavender. Momma's gonna go see Gypsy, then the doctor."

"Gypsy," Gracie repeated.

"You two finish your wagon ride. I'll check in later."

Matt asked if the girls had seen me fall. Maria shook her head. Then he helped me into the truck. Maggie and Glad rode in the back seat. No one said a word during the short drive. Tristan strolled out of the barn with a long face. We didn't have many days like this on the ranch, and this really sucked.

"Mom and I will wait out here," Maggie said.

"I'd like to hear what Trout has to say," Glad said.

"You sure?" I didn't want her to see me cry, and judging by the sting behind my eyes, tears were inescapable. I took Glad's hand when she offered it to me.

"You couldn't keep me away with a stick. Let me be here for you." Glad squeezed my fingers.

"It's that easy," Matt said.

Shafts of golden sun and the aromas of leather and hay greeted us. Peeking into the stall, I held my breath. Trout crouched next to Gypsy and examined her front legs.

"Girl, it's a miracle you're not more banged up." Trout stood. "You know the score. My guess is a tendon." His scruffy white chin gleamed in the light.

"She has to be fine." I clenched my fists.

"She needs time. I've called Sarah," he said.

"Please, girl, you've got to make it. I'll sleep out here if I have to."

"Oh Lord. You can't be sleeping in the barn with Gypsy. You've got your own healing to do."

"I'll do whatever it takes to get her better."

"Kid, you know how this goes."

"Yes. I do, but I'm not willing to let go. When have I ever been willing to let go?" I bit my lip. My gaze met Matt's. He was *my* cowboy, my heart.

"That's my girl," Glad said.

"You girls are all cut from the same cloth." Trout stepped out of the stall and latched the door.

"Spirits travel in packs, old man. You know that better than anyone," Glad said.

"Who you calling old man?" Trout produced a pack of smokes from the breast pocket of his coat. "This is gonna be a long haul."

CHAPTER 13

D AD DROVE ALONG the winding road with exceeding caution. Doc Porter's office was five miles behind us, and home seemed like days away. I stared out the passenger window, praying for Gypsy, then for myself.

"I told you nothing was broken. And those new machines of his got quite the workout." I paused. "The bruises will go away. He said there weren't any signs of a concussion."

"All I'm saying is, take it easy for a bit. Let Matt do the heavy lifting when it comes to organizing the wranglers. Anything with the horses or the barns can wait. You've got Maria, and Red is here."

"He's already doing that." I stared at Dad's twitching temple. "Nothing will *ever* be the same if I have to put her down." Who would I tell my secrets to? I needed my girl now more than ever.

"Let the vet do her thing, and you worry about you."

"Easier said than done, Dad. I think we both

know that. Gypsy feels everything I feel, knows me better than I know myself, and loves me on good days and bad." Wetness stained my cheeks. "She's not just a horse."

"I know, Chloe. We'll do everything we can. Gypsy's not the only one who loves you on good days and bad."

"Regardless, I'm proof that animals are imperative to human development and emotional needs. I need you to get on board with providing for others."

Dad pulled into the drive, stopped on the bridge, got out of the truck, and stared at the river. I, too, got out and listened to the river's song. Leaning against the rail, I stared into the ripples of water rushing beneath me. Dad kicked at the dusty planks, then wrapped his arm around my shoulders.

"I don't know anyone like you. You're a prize-fighter with a pretty face."

"Is there any other way to be?"

"We all have plenty of choices," he said.

"Not for me. My motto isn't flight or fight. It's fight or fight harder." I held my dad's gaze. "Who do you think I learned it from?" A cool rush of air kissed my neck, and the scent of Grandpa's cigarettes drifted past. "I'll be okay. I need Gypsy to be okay, too. I've had worse scrapes than this. Remember the time I slid down the hillside into the east pasture? You picked thorns from my skin along with embedded pebbles. I still have the scar on my arm." I rolled up my sleeve to show him.

"And I slid down behind trying to catch you."

"You were a real-life hero—"

"—attempting to save my damsel in distress. I don't like it when people get hurt on my watch." Dad dropped his chin with a heavy breath. "Can you please stay off a horse for a few days and rest like Doc Porter said? You're gonna be sore."

"I'm not gonna promise."

Dad kissed my cheek.

"Love you, too," I said. "I meant what I said about Gypsy. She's more than a horse. She's my soul sister, my savior. You just can't see her angel wings, and there are many more like her."

"What would I do without you, Chloe?"

"I don't know." I forced a toothy grin and lifted my chin to the beating sun riding high in the sky. "Thanks for taking care of me, Dad."

"Anytime." He escorted me back to the truck.

Maggie, Glad, Maria, Red, and Matt waited on the porch with Lil and Gracie. Dad smiled. "Now that's a welcoming committee."

"Sure is." I pointed to the pickup parked in the

drive near the barn. "Sarah is here. Can you drive me to the barn?"

"Sure. Better tell the girls where you're headed." Dad parked in front of the main house.

I got out of the truck. Matt skipped down the steps and took me in his arms.

"Nothing is broken. Got some bruises. No concussion. I'm fine. Mostly." What I thought was relief washed over Glad and Red's expressions. Maggie held my stare as if she wasn't quite convinced. Maria gave me a thumbs-up, then continued playing with the girls. "Dad's gonna drive me to the barn."

"Thank the Lord. You scared me to death." Matt glanced over to my dad. "I'll take her, John."

"The keys are in the truck," Dad said. "Come on, girls. We'll walk and talk."

Matt buckled me into the passenger's seat and shut the door. Dad gestured for me to roll the window down.

"Whatever Sarah says goes. Are you ready for that?"

"Ready as I'll ever be." I sat a bit taller after Dad's reassuring pat on the shoulder.

I watched Glad, Maggie, Red, and Maria, in the side-view mirror as Matt pulled away from the house. The women strode together, leading the way for Gracie and Lil. We were a force to be reckoned with. Dad brought up the rear, picking dandelions along the way for the girls like the champion pop-pop that he was.

"You're one tough nut," Matt said.

"It's a gift." I tried to smile.

"When I saw you go down, my heart stopped."

Goose bumps covered my arms. *His heart stopped for you. He loves you, girl.*

"I'm glad you're okay. The girls and I need you. And that's all I'm gonna say, 'cause there's a group of people heading this way." Matt parked close to the barn.

"Thanks, Matt. I need—" Before I could finish my thought of needing him, too, he cut me off.

"We can talk later."

We got out of the truck, waited for Dad, then went into the barn together. Gypsy's injury meant she'd be stall-bound for a while. Sarah explained a regimen for cold therapy to manage swelling, as well as anti-inflammatory and pain meds for the damaged tendon. Dad crossed his arms over his chest. Trout nodded along. Maggie, Glad, Red, and the girls waited outside, then joined us after we'd finished talking.

My heart fluttered when Matt picked up Lil. There wasn't anything sexier than a cowboy holding a child. By the expression on Sarah's face, she liked a cowboy holding a child, too.

"So you're saying Gypsy's got a chance?" I crossed my fingers.

Gracie reached for me, and I took her from Maggie. Gracie pressed her cheek into the crook of my neck and hugged me. My gaze met Matt's. Hopefully, he and I had a chance, too.

"It depends on her and how patient she is, and we all know animals have a mind of their own. The healing process is lengthy, could take six months to a year, and even then, she may not be able to use that leg like she has been." Sarah ran her fingers through Gypsy's tangled mane. "At some point, we can do physical therapy."

Lord knew, Gypsy was as strong-willed as I was. Gracie put her cheek next to mine, where I could feel her soft breaths. Every creature was the master of their being. I couldn't make Gypsy heal any more than Dad could get me to stay off a horse.

"We'll do our best," I said.

Maggie and Red watched on, wide-eyed. Gracie tickled my neck. Someday she'd be standing in this barn with *her* horse. Lil, too.

"You know horses, but I thought this information might help." Sarah pulled a trifold packet of papers from her back pocket and handed them to Dad. I traded Gracie for the papers. Her eyes lit up when her pop-pop held her.

"So you'll be back soon?" I asked.

"Yes, I've been asked to check in tomorrow. I'd like to do everything I can to make her a success story."

"Me too," I said.

"Besides, Emma wants to see Huckleberry." Sarah packed up her portable ultrasound scanner and gathered her things.

Sarah had given Gypsy a chance.

Suddenly aware of my heartbeat, I stroked Gypsy's hide, then produced a piece of sugar from my pocket. She ate it, lowered her head, and closed her eyes. *If there was ever a time to be cooperative, it would be now.*

"Call me if you have any questions." Sarah peeked into Gypsy's stall one last time before Dad and Trout escorted her to her truck.

"Momma." Lil laid her head on Gypsy.

"Girls—looks like we might be momma-less for a bit longer." Worry rimmed Matt's eyes. "Which one of you fine ladies would like to take this little one so I can get back to work?"

Maggie swooped in.

"You okay, Chloe?" Glad stepped closer.

"For now. I suspect I'll be praying more than usual. Patience isn't my forte."

"We all will. We know how important Gypsy is to you." She pushed the orange speckled glasses balanced at the tip of her nose to the top of her head. "Faith is invisible. Lean into it, girl."

"I will."

"You're a good momma."

"I love my horses."

"I'm not just talking about the horses."

"I know, Gladiola." I watched Matt ride away on Trigger. Maggie pulled the girls' wagon, and Red strolled alongside. "I love my girls. The circle keeps growing." I held Glad's hand. Her touch hadn't aged even if she had.

"And you love Matt." She paused. "Perfect timing doesn't have to be a twist of fate."

CHAPTER 14

SLEEPING ON A cot in the barn wasn't exactly part of Doc Porter's orders or what Matt meant when he'd reminded me of my duties. This morning, I'd woken up about 4:00 a.m., gone back to the house, and found Matt standing in the kitchen drinking coffee.

"I get that you're worried about Gypsy." He rubbed his brow. "Should've known you were serious about sleeping in the barn. What'll be next?"

"What's with the tone?"

"I'm being as patient as I can." His temple twitched. "There's a lot going on here. Bradley and Red, the reno, now Gypsy. There's no time for us. Branch offered me a job in Wyoming, and I accepted."

"You can't be serious." I took off my beanie and barn coat. A pain rippled through my torso as I slipped my arms out of the sleeves.

"What about the girls? What about us?"

Matt set his coffee cup on the counter.

"When we met in college, you told me you didn't need anyone, and I was good with that because I didn't need anyone either. That understanding made it easy to get close to you," he explained.

"And now you want it all." My gaze met his.

"I do. Turns out, I'm more traditional than I thought. I didn't want you hearing about Branch's offer from anyone else. You once asked me what I feared most."

"And you said regret. We were at a crossroads. Seems we're there again."

"Nothing good comes from forcing an issue or creating a contract in an effort to avoid hurt. Those circumstances aren't created from the love I know. I never thought I'd go to Wyoming, but maybe the distance between us will put things in perspective, help us move forward without each other."

Matt smoothed my hair back, and I rested my hands on his hips.

"The Chloe McIntyre I know is fearless."

"I guess I fooled you."

"If that were the case, Chloe, I wouldn't be standing here. I would've left a long time ago."

"If that was the case, Matt Cooper, you wouldn't have told me you wanted to marry me.

You would've just proposed. We were both testing the waters."

I SAT AT my desk, leafing through articles of successful animal therapy centers. When I dialed my mother, she answered on the second ring.

"Hi, Mom." I caressed the framed photo of Gypsy sitting on my desk.

"Is something wrong?"

"Why?" I moved papers, then played with the old horseshoe I dug from the ground the day Gypsy and I fell. Tristan warned me, and I didn't listen.

"You never call in the middle of the morning. Shouldn't you be out with the cattle?" She shushed someone speaking in the background and asked them to give her five minutes.

"I'm just working at my desk. Thinking."

"Sounds serious. How are my girls?"

"Lil and Grace are good. More teeth. They're outside with Maria."

"Tell them Coco sends her love." My mother the fashionista had chosen the nickname Coco after the girls were born. The thought of being called Grannie or Grandma was a *no can do.*

She cleared her voice. "Why are you working

inside? What's wrong?"

"Gypsy and I had a fall." I raked my fingers through my hair.

"Are you hurt?"

"I'm okay. Just banged up." I went to the window and put my hand on the cool glass. "I'm worried Gypsy won't make it. I've been sleeping in the barn with her."

"How's Matt feel about that?"

I hesitated. "He doesn't like it. He thinks I should focus on myself." My words meant nothing now that he'd hired on with Branch.

"Ah! There it is. Just a second. It's crazy here."

I sighed. "When have I ever been able to *focus on myself?* How is that even possible?" I nibbled on my thumbnail.

"What distractions are there *now?*" Mom asked.

"I thought you put me on hold. I was talking to myself."

"Apparently. What gives?"

"Bradley is getting married. He and his fiancée, Red, want to have their wedding at the ranch. I said I'd help. And—I'm not sure I should say."

"Tell Bradley congratulations. That's big of you to help. Suspicious, I'd almost say, but I'm sure Maggie is over the moon."

I nibbled on the other thumbnail. If anyone understood my feelings about not wanting to get married, it would be my mom. "Matt says he wants to get married. That's not what we agreed on. Now he thinks putting some distance between us might help put things in perspective. I'm more mixed up than ever."

"To be honest, I saw it coming, and I thought you would, too."

I pinched the bridge of my nose, this morning's conversation fresh in my mind.

"Chloe, I'm sure you'll work it out."

"We both know this is a slippery slope, Mom. Saying *I do* can only lead to one thing, and I think you know what that is. We're fighting already." Mom didn't respond, and I tapped the screen of my phone, thinking the call had cut out. "Hello?"

"I'm here. I heard you. Chloe, not everyone gets divorced. Everything has its risks."

I paced.

"Chloe, are you there?"

"Yes, Mom. I've got a few things to tie up before I head out this afternoon. Red's looking for a wedding dress."

"You called for a reason. Don't change the subject. Just because your father and I got divorced doesn't mean you will."

"If we're being honest, I'm more like you than we'll both admit. There are things I want to do, accomplish—and I'm not sure I can, being hitched."

"If that were true, you wouldn't have called. You'll accomplish anything you set out to do. Your situation is different from mine and your dad's. You called for support and you've got it. You're both where you're supposed to be if you ask me."

"But Matt and I agreed not to marry." Irritation laced my words.

"People change their minds. Feelings change."

"Apparently." And after she'd married my dad, their feelings *changed* big-time. Featherstone and his work crew pulled into the drive. "Mr. Featherstone is here. I've gotta go."

"Did you choose the trough sink we discussed?"

"Yup. And the work is going faster than expected."

"That's great. I can't wait to see it."

"I can't wait for you to see it, too. Do you know anything about writing grants?"

"Why?"

"Long story."

"Give me the short version."

"I want to open an animal therapy center on the ranch for children with emotional issues. Writing a grant would help me get it off the ground. Dad only sees numbers. I see opportunity. I see a bigger purpose."

"That's my girl." She chuckled. "That's wonderful, Chloe. Listen, Hermione is calling on the other line. I'll call you back later? We're trying to finalize the details for our next collection."

"Sure, Mom. Tell Hermione I said hello."

"I will. Love you, daughter."

"Love you back."

"Have fun shopping. I know a fashionista who can help Red with a wedding dress if she doesn't find anything. Hermione and I are cooking up a spring bridal edition for the magazine, and Red should participate. We've got some spectacular gowns. And, Chloe, no more falls, okay?"

"I'll do my best, Mom."

MAGGIE, GLAD, RED, and I drove into Bozeman on a wedding dress quest. Red wasn't set on any particular style, and visiting trendy boutiques suited her.

At the first wedding shop, Red had tried on ten gowns, twirled on a pedestal, and made it clear she could shop all day. On our way to the second boutique, Maggie and Glad ducked into the furniture store next door to see a studded coffee table in the window that Maggie said was calling her name.

Sweet scents of fresh flowers and soft perfume greeted Red and me at the door, along with a blonde in a black cocktail dress with scorching maroon lips. She introduced herself as Rebecca, not of Sunnybrook Farm. She led us into a sea of organza, silk, and gowns layered in puffy fancy fabric that reminded me of Glad's lemon meringue pie.

I fingered a beaded belt on an elegant dress with an empire waist. "Have you seen anything you like?"

"I like the off-the-shoulder column gown at the last place the best." Red pulled a lacy mermaid dress from the wall fixture, inspecting the possibility in the mirror. "Too frilly."

"There sure is a lot to choose from. Boston must have hundreds of stores and options." I showed her a silky gown with spaghetti straps.

"Looks like a negligee," Red said.

"At least you could wear it again." I held it up to myself and posed in the mirror. "Totally." I put it back on the rack. "Can I ask you a personal question?"

"Sure, shoot." Red fingered the skirt of a fussy dress dotted with crystals and sequins.

"Do you and Bradley argue?"

"Not often, but sure. I heard Matt talking to Tristan in the barn yesterday." She tucked long tendrils of hair behind her ears. Her complexion glowed.

"What were they talking about? I can take it. It might hurt worse than falling off Gypsy, but I need to know what he's thinking. We're not on the same page."

Rebecca showed Red a sleek column gown similar to the one she liked in the first store. Red caressed the silky fabric and requested to try it on.

"I'm not sure it's my place, Chloe. Maybe you should talk to Matt."

I sighed. She was right. I moved to the next rack of gowns, chose a very traditional ball gown, and held it next to Red. She was timeless, classic. I was not.

"This is beautiful. See, you can pick out dresses." Red held the gown and stared into a trifold mirror.

"Wish I had your girly-ness," I said.

"You do."

In the mirror, I compared myself to this city girl

who loved my brother. "I don't think I do. Look at us. We're as different as can be. My mother would love shopping with you. And by the way, I spoke to her this morning. If you're up to it, she's planning a bridal spread in her magazine and would like you to take part. What do you think?"

"I think I could be talked into that. Sounds fun." Red hung the gown on the dressing room door, then disappeared behind an overflowing rack of chiffon and lace.

Rebecca added two more wedding dresses to the dressing room. "I'll be back in a few minutes to check in. Can I get you something to drink?"

"Do you have a shot and a beer?" By the expression on her face, she didn't think my request was amusing. "Sorry, we'll let you know when you check back. Thank you."

Rebecca patted my arm. "I see it all the time. Don't worry. Your day will come."

"Will it now?" My sarcasm cut the quiet ambiance, but not her happy-as-a-clam disposition.

"I've been helping brides for more than twenty years." Rebecca's perfect teeth gleamed. She clasped her hands at her waist, her shoulders taut with confidence.

"Really?" With a hard stare, I inspected her perfect complexion.

"I'll be back." She turned on a heel and scurried off.

"Like the Terminator?" I muttered to myself. I stood on the pedestal and imagined I was Red. Designer dresses and elegant notions I hadn't dreamed of swept me away. I took the bandanna from my back pocket and tied it around my head like a rocker-chick. "That's more like it," I said to myself. Scrolling the internet for pictures and wedding ideas was easier than living it firsthand. Finishing this project was just as important as anything else I worked for.

Red appeared from nowhere, and I slid the bandanna from my head. Where'd you go?" My words wobbled with nervous vibrato. "Rebecca was here. She brought more gowns."

"I want you to be my maid of honor. It would mean a lot to Bradley and me."

As I stepped down, my brow twitched like it did when I'd gotten caught in a fib or had to take a test. "I'm sure you have girlfriends who would jump at the chance."

Red's stare intensified. "I choose you."

My eyes brimmed with tears, not from sheer joy but from the confusion of what I wanted and lack of sleep. I dabbed my eyes with my bandanna. "I can't believe I'm crying."

"It's okay. You're pretty tired, and you've got a lot on your mind with the twins, the barn, and the therapy center."

"I'm more than tired." I started laughing. "Finally, a girl who gets me." I thought it best to leave Matt out of the conversation.

"Chloe, you're whacky like Bradley said, but to know you is to love you. What do you say? Be my maid of honor."

"I don't want you to disappoint your friends."

"My friends won't be disappointed. They don't roll that way."

Red took a veil from a rack, put it on, and fluffed the fine lace.

Rebecca returned with an armful of dresses for me to try on. "These come in an array of colors." She opened the door to a dressing room next to the one she'd set up for Red. "Let me know if I can get you ladies anything else. We *do* have sparkling wine."

"That would be lovely," I said.

"Thank you. A midafternoon cocktail sounds wonderful." Red returned the veil to the rack.

Rebecca smiled, turned on a heel, and sauntered away.

I inspected the crystal princess tiaras displayed in a fancy glass cabinet. "Lil and Grace would love these."

"I'm having so much fun. Thanks for making everything so special."

"You're welcome. You're as cool as a cucumber."

"Nothing to be intimidated by. The wine is coming. I'll try on the gown you picked out, and you choose something from the dresses Rebecca hung in your room." Red put on a pillbox hat with a veil not big enough to cover a grapefruit. "Very forties. Reminds me of those black-and-white movies I used to watch with my uncle. He wasn't much into princesses or romcoms."

I went into the dressing room. Caressing the midnight-colored fabric, I kicked off my boots and wiggled out of my designer jeans and into a strapless, form-fitting number.

"Come out, Chloe. I want to see what you have on," Red said.

I peeked out. Glad and Maggie lounged on the pink velvet sofa, sipping wine. "That must've been some coffee table."

"We thought you two girls would like some time alone. We're the party crashers. And now we're sipping your wine." Maggie made a toast to love and clinked her glass with Glad's.

"You're hardly party crashers. Come *all* the

way out, Chloe." Glad adjusted the zebra-printed reading glasses at the end of her nose.

"I don't want to." I opened the dressing room door. My gaze fell on Red, who stood on a riser, inspecting herself. "Um, how did Bradley get so lucky? You're beautiful."

"Chloe, this is a gorgeous gown. You've got a great sense of design. Your mom would definitely be impressed."

"Yes, she would. But you've got the body."

"The dress is perfect." Maggie set her glass of wine on the table next to the box of tissues.

"It sure is," I said, fingering the silk flowing down around Red like a waterfall of lusciousness. "I love how you pinned your hair up. Very elegant."

Glad reached across Maggie for the tissue box.

Red pulled me up on the riser next to her. My dress? Not exactly what I'd imagined myself wearing, ever. "This looked so much better on the hanger. My barely there chest is quite on display." I pulled at the clinging bodice crushing my sore rib cage.

"Try another one." Red shooed me away.

I scooted back into my dressing room, rearranged the hangers, not connecting with any of my choices. Then Rebecca slipped a free-flowing gown

I'd seen in one of Red's bridal magazines into my room. It was the gown I'd choose if I were the one getting married. It wasn't traditional. It was Chloe.

I wiggled out of the nightmare I had on and stepped into the creamy bohemian gown. My heart raced. I held my hair up at the nape of my neck, then let it fall freely over my shoulders.

"Come out, Chloe," Red said through the slats of the dressing room door.

I opened the door. Red's smile gave me goose bumps. I showed Maggie and Glad the dress. "This isn't appropriate."

Red modeled a strapless gown with a tailored skirt. A lacy train pooled around her feet. She'd pinned a short, sleek veil in her hair.

"Breathtaking," Maggie said.

"You two are gorgeous brides," Glad added. "To the brides-to-be."

"I think you've had enough to drink, Gladiola." I reached for her glass, but she drank what was left before I could take it.

Stepping onto the riser, I admired the tatted lace sewn into the free-flowing skirt and wispy flowing fabric of the dress I modeled. The plunging keyhole of the halter-like top was alluring, the straps tied at my nape the color of golden honey. A twinge of jealousy caught me by surprise when I glanced at Red, and I pushed it down. How could I envy something I never wanted?

CHAPTER 15

D RESS SHOPPING HAD ended on a high note at the third boutique. Glad had strutted around, twirled, and claimed she'd missed her calling as a model as she tried on mother-of-the-bride dresses. I reassured her I had an in if she really wanted to walk the runway.

Back home, I dropped Maggie, Glad, and Red at the main house. I parked the truck and went inside to check on Maria and the girls. "Hello," I called from the kitchen.

Maria appeared with an empty laundry basket tucked beneath her arm. "Hey. The girls are sleeping. I'm waiting for a load of towels."

"Something smells great." I turned on the oven light.

"I'm working on a batch of cookies. I know there's leftover birthday cake, but who doesn't like a bite-sized peanut butter treat? Perfect for the girls. Hope that's okay."

The young woman before me had her life together. She worked, problem solved, could handle the girls and our crazy schedule.

"You're spoiling me."

"My pleasure."

"I'm gonna check on Gypsy."

"Since the girls are sleeping, is it okay if I do some schoolwork?"

"Of course. How'd that last project go?"

"I got an A. I just have some reading to do."

"Enjoy." I said goodbye and went to the barn.

Matt slung his saddle on the rack in the tack room with a grunt. Dust billowed outside the barn door, and the sun cut through the clouds.

Shuffling over, not sure what to say, I studied his profile. Trigger shuffled to the side and bobbed his head in Matt's direction.

"Do you need something, Chloe?"

"Thought I'd help you clean up."

"Thought you were shopping with Red." He tossed a coiled rope atop the tack box.

"I can leave if I'm in the way." I peeked into Gypsy's stall. She greeted me with a whinny, and I fed her the two carrots I'd snapped in half.

"If you've got something to say, say it." Matt planted his hands on his hips.

"What do you want me to say?"

"That you've come to your senses. I've spent the day thinking about Branch's offer and us." His stoic stare was uncharacteristic.

"Come to my senses concerning what? You've made your decision."

"Guess you haven't. I've got work, Chloe." He took off his gloves and massaged his temples. "Being at odds isn't good for either one of us or the girls."

As much as I wanted to tell him to renege on Branch's offer, I didn't. He'd made his decision. I kicked the tack box and left. Gusts of warm air caught my cowboy hat. It skipped across the ground, and I hurried to catch it. Dad rode toward me. I snagged my hat and peered up at him. "What's going on? This wind is nuts."

"You'd better get back to the house." Dad pointed to the ominous clouds moving in. "Get going. You should be with Gracie and Lil. You know how much they love a good storm."

Tristan, Quinn, Silas, and Justin rode in from the horizon. They cantered across the field in our direction.

"Maybe I should stay here and help batten down the hatches." But by the look in Dad's eyes, I had one place to be, and it wasn't with the men. Fine. Hair swirled around my face. I lowered my chin, held my hat, and walked into the wind. I thought I heard Matt calling my name. When I turned to look, no one was there.

Maria stood by her car. "Glad and Red are inside with the girls. Maggie told me to get going. Is that okay?"

"Of course. Be careful driving home."

The back door of the house rattled when I closed it. I straightened the mudroom cluttered with boots and jackets. Glad's singing drifted through the kitchen. She and Red played in the living room with the girls. Lil reached for me the second our gazes met, and Gracie played on the floor like she didn't have a care in the world.

"It's okay, Lil. Momma is home."

Red stacked blocks and Gracie knocked them down. "Ashes, ashes, they all fall down," Red sang.

"Again." Gracie clapped with excitement.

Red glanced out the window, then ruffled Gracie's hair. "Maybe I should go up to the main house to see if Maggie needs help with dinner now that you're back."

"Glad, you want to go, too?" I asked.

"No, I'll stay and keep you company."

"You don't have to." The truth was, I wanted to be left alone with the girls. Matt's intensity bothered me. The evening ahead promised uncertainty.

"Come on, girls. It's dinner time." I helped Lil to the kitchen and set her in one of the high chairs.

"There you go, G." Red hooked Gracie into the other high chair. "Thanks again for the shopping trip today. I haven't had that much fun in a long time."

"You're welcome. I had a great time, too." I sprinkled a few bite-size cheesy crackers on the girls' trays. "Maggie and Glad got a kick out of seeing us in all those dresses."

I could feel the hard line in the seam of my lips steal my smile. Lil stared at me with her daddy's dark eyes.

Glad joined us and looked out the kitchen window. Worry framed her solemn gaze. "Sure is nasty out there." She drummed her fingers on the counter.

"We're having roasted chicken and vegetables for dinner." I picked out the carrots and sweet potatoes for the girls.

"I'll have a little. I eat like a bird. A nibble here, a nibble there." Glad chuckled. "I think the wine I had in town went to my head."

"You're right about that," I said.

"What's the long face for?"

"Change sucks."

"I know." Glad sat at the kitchen table. She

fidgeted with the ceramic salt and pepper shakers shaped like chickens.

Peeking out the kitchen window, I scanned the landscape shadowed by angry clouds.

"How are those ribs of yours?"

I rubbed my side, then pressed a smidge harder. "Pretty much normal, but they sure did ache earlier in the week."

"As much as a broken heart?" Glad straightened the silverware and handed the girls the toddler forks they were learning to use.

Lil and Gracie babbled and played with the measuring cups I'd given them until their veggies cooled. Gracie's shrill shriek pierced the air. Lil covered her ears, and I calmed her.

"What's with the broken heart comment?" I asked.

"Broken hearts don't always mend. Is that a risk you're willing to take? You sure looked beautiful in that long gauzy gown today."

A gust of wind slammed against the side of the house, making the windows rattle. My heart jumped with the startle. Lil inspected me with wide eyes. She chewed faster after the crack of thunder. Gracie ate her dinner, pretending not to hear the storm.

"My heart's not broken, Gladiola. And you're

starting to sound like Trout." I gave the girls the veggies.

"Maybe not yet. Today, there was something in your eyes I'd never seen. It was love, dear girl." She helped Lil manage her carrots.

My shoulders slumped forward as I dropped the dish towel on the counter. Rain dripped like a slow leaking faucet outside, then there was another clap of thunder.

"Today *was* a lot of fun." I couldn't look at Glad.

She stood, wrapped her arm around my waist, and drew me close.

"Red and Bradley make a perfect couple. They deserve every happiness in the world," I said.

"And so do you. Good grief. You're denser than one of my mother's loaves of bread."

I held her stare, waiting for a lecture.

"That's all I have to say." She took off her reading glasses.

Rain pelted the rooftop.

"I hope the guys got their horses settled," I said.

"I'm sure they're fine." Glad ate a potato from Lil's plate. "Watching these two eat is making me hungry."

The back door slammed shut. Matt stood in the

doorway to the mudroom, kicked off his boots, and hung up his raincoat. He told Lola to sit, and she did until he wiped her down.

"What's the matter?" I leaned against the counter, a knot in my belly.

"Your dad was checking on Gypsy. A wicked gust blew through, and she freaked out. He tried getting out of the way but ended up face down in the floorboards. He's got a gash in his forehead. He cleaned it up, then showed me how to apply the butterfly strips." Matt rubbed away the tension in his jaw. "It's brutal out there."

"Did Gypsy settle down?"

"Yes. Glad can stay with us if the weather doesn't stop."

"Great, a sleepover." She helped Lil finish her dinner, then gave her a peanut butter cookie.

Matt ducked out of the kitchen, and I followed. He put his elbow on the mantel and took off his cowboy hat. "I think we should talk after everyone is in bed," he said.

I turned away. Where were we headed? Wherever it was—made me nervous. "Can I get you some dinner?"

"Sure." Matt plopped down on the sofa and propped his feet up on the ottoman.

Lil toddled in, happy to see her daddy. She

worked her way up into his lap. Her sparkling gaze put the storm in perspective. Lola jumped up on the sofa next to them and snuggled in with a soft snore.

"Is GLAD ALL tucked in?" Matt sounded tired and half asleep.

"Yup. I love having her around, but now that she's getting older, she's changing. I don't like it." I crawled over him and under the covers. "She's moving slower. Her appetite isn't as hearty."

"We can't stay young forever. There's a ticking clock, Chloe." Matt's scruffy tone sounded irritated.

"I tried on dresses with Red today."

"Let's not talk about weddings." The sharp line of his jaw was all telling. "It's clear we both want different things," he said.

"I'm surprised you took Branch's offer." I wrapped my arms around myself.

"We see different futures, Chloe. I'm sorry."

"Can't we talk about it?" I held his gaze.

"It's been a long day. I'm glad you had a good time shopping. Maria and Emma were good with the girls. Good night, Chloe."

I propped myself up on my elbows. "Emma

was here?"

"Sarah stopped by to check on Gypsy after you left. Emma had a good time with Lil and Gracie. Seems she likes little girls as well as horses. Sarah and Emma will be back, day after tomorrow." Matt raked his fingers through his messy hair and yawned.

"This is why we need that animal therapy center." I kicked off the covers and sat up.

"Switching gears is so easy for you. You're missing the scenery."

"Missing the scenery? Seriously." My voice was shrill.

"Ssssh. You'll wake the girls and Glad."

"Are you kidding me?" I climbed into Matt's lap, straddled his thighs, and blew hair away from my face. "Why can't we talk?"

"If this is your way of apologizing, it's not very becoming." He glanced at the clock.

The floorboards outside our room creaked, and we stopped bickering. I hopped out of bed and tiptoed toward the light creeping beneath the door. I peeked into the hallway. Glad stood there in flannel pajamas looking confused. "What's the matter, Gladiola?"

"Is the storm over? I thought I could sleep here, but I'm not so sure. I like my bed at Maggie's. Are these my pajamas?"

"I'm sorry we woke you. It's still raining." I held her hand. She knew she'd borrowed a pair of my pajamas. Was she sleepwalking? "I'll walk you to the main house if you want, but I wish you'd stay."

"Does Maggie know I'm here?"

"She does." I patted Glad's hand. "Are you okay?"

"Maybe I should stay put. Morning will be here soon. Right?" Glad's fraught gaze flickered.

"Yes, it will," Matt said from behind me. "I'm sorry we woke you."

"I can't sleep." Glad headed back to her room.

"You're safe here." I helped her get situated in bed, kissed her cheek, smoothed hair away from her face, and sat with her.

"You're sweet. You really should quit quarreling with Matt. Nothing good comes from going to bed angry."

"How long were you in the hallway?"

"Long enough." She pulled the quilt up to her chin and fidgeted with the covers.

Matt appeared in the doorway.

"I'll stay with her," I said.

He said good night and turned out the hallway light. I held Glad's hand until she fell asleep.

When Matt and I moved in together, we had agreed not to go to sleep angry, but we'd said lots of things. I knew he'd be snoring by the time I got back to bed, and sure enough, he was. I went downstairs to my office and shut the French doors. Blinking away sleep, I rested my head on the desk. Tangled emotions resulted in a weighing knot of sleepless worry.

CHAPTER 16

I'D GONE TO the barn around eleven after the rain stopped, talked to Gypsy, and fallen asleep on the cot outside her stall. I woke to the eerie sound in the rafters about an hour later, said goodnight to my girl, hurried home, and checked on Glad, who was sound asleep.

The girls and I woke at the crack of dawn. As much as I wanted to run the horses with the crew, I didn't. I needed my space, and so did Matt. Funny thing about being on this ranch—for as much land as we owned, when things got uncomfortable, the sprawling acres closed in on me.

The sun came up as if a storm hadn't existed. The girls and I walked Glad back to the main house after breakfast. Her spunk and vigor had returned as if last night hadn't occurred.

I thought about Red and Bradley. The elegant dresses we tried on yesterday. The linen invitations Red chose. The scent of a locker full of fresh blooms at Maggie's favorite florist. Glad sipping sparkling wine and showing off her eighty-nine-year-old figure at the boutique. The attention on Red. The attention I was happy to stay clear of until I tried on that dress. The argument with Matt had squelched the feelings I'd been avoiding.

I reminded myself no two journeys were the same even if two people traveled together or settled on a forever agreement. Settling seemed deflating. Settling made for safe surroundings. Settling veiled importance. What kind of compromise was left now that Matt would be working in Wyoming?

When Matt and I had moved in together, it hadn't felt like settling. I thought we'd gotten our happily ever after.

Maggie and Red sat side by side in the rocking chairs on the porch of the main house, sipping tea.

"Hey, Maggie. What's on your agenda today?" I picked Lil up, making sure Gracie didn't fall backward as she climbed the stairs.

"Why? What do you have in mind?"

"I thought we could pack up the girls and hitch up the horses for a wagon ride. Maria has the day off. What do you think?"

"We could do that." Maggie didn't sound so eager to leave the house.

"If you're busy, no worries."

"Don't you need to be around for Mr. Feather-stone?"

"I'll check in with him when he gets here. His team is finishing floorboards today. I think they're working on skylights next. How's Dad?"

"He's fine. In case you've forgotten, *he is* a doctor." She sighed. "I'd feel better if someone checked him out. Matt did a fine job with those butterfly strips."

"Did you check his pupils? Wake him up?"

"Yes. I woke him up in the middle of the night. That didn't go over well."

"It's good to be back home." Glad patted Maggie's arm, then went inside.

"Speaking of waking up in the middle of the night." I sat next to Maggie, glanced over my shoulder to make sure Glad wasn't lurking. "Glad woke up last night. I found her in the hallway. She seemed confused, not her usual self. I wanted to let you know. I sat with her until she fell asleep. The storm scared her. She wanted to come home. She's been at my house during storms plenty of times."

"Age does things to us." Maggie sipped her tea.

Lil climbed into Red's lap. Gracie laid next to Samson and petted his thick head.

"How bad is it?" I leaned closer to Maggie.

"At her last physical, the doctor didn't seem too concerned yet. She told me there's medication if we wanted. Most the time, Mom seems fine.

We've had a few incidents, too. Usually when the sun goes down. I'll make another appointment. Thanks for letting me know."

Glad joined us on the porch with a cup of tea. We rocked in the warm morning sunshine until Maggie set her cup down, took in the fresh air, then announced there were more wedding plans to attend to before we could spend the day playing.

Mr. Featherstone and his crew pulled in the drive and headed to the barn.

"That's my cue." I took the bandanna from my back pocket and tied it around my head. "Can the girls hang with you until I'm done? After talking to Mr. Featherstone, I'll check on the wranglers, then be back."

Tristan rode Casanova past the house. I whistled at him. Casanova looked mighty fine these days and acted like he'd been tame his whole life. Tristan pulled back on the reins. The Appaloosa stood on hind legs, showing off his sleek black socks and spots.

"Show-off," I said, getting to my feet, and skipping down the stairs.

"What's up, bosslady?"

"Just thought I might bend your ear on the way to the barn." I blew the girls a kiss and waved goodbye.

Tristan had Casanova bow on command. Gracie clapped.

"They're gonna think all the animals can do tricks." I peered up at Tristan. "You look different today. In a good way."

"The soap and water in the bunkhouse must be working."

"That's not what I mean. What gives?"

Sarah drove up the drive.

"I thought she was coming by tomorrow to check on Gypsy." I shaded my brow. "I guess it's more than the soap and water."

"I don't know what you mean."

"I think you do. Let's walk and talk." I patted Casanova's neck. "I hear Emma had a good time with the girls yesterday."

Sarah parked her truck. Emma opened the passenger's side door and ran toward the fence. My heart pinched when Huckleberry trotted over to meet her. Sarah waved hello.

"Since Maria's off today, I'll be with the girls. I'll have the radio if you need me." Tristan didn't respond, so I fed Casanova the sugar from my pocket. Suspicion arose when he didn't razz me about sugary treats. "Your pants are on fire, and that soap and water really isn't working. I'll just take Casanova to market. Maybe trade him for an elk loin and a bottle of whiskey."

Tristan tied Casanova to the hitching post.

"Is that okay with you, cowboy?"

"Did you say something, bosslady?"

I pulled him aside. "Sarah's mighty pretty."

He dropped his chin.

"She's here to see you, isn't she?"

"Don't know."

"I doubt that," I said. "I need to check in with Featherstone. But before I do, I'm gonna say hello to Emma."

"Hey, there." Sarah tucked her long dark hair behind her ears.

"Good morning. Thought you were coming tomorrow to see Gypsy."

"Yeah, I'll be out tomorrow, too. Emma really wanted to see Huckleberry. I hope you don't mind."

"Of course I don't." I kept an eye on Emma. "Thanks for letting Emma spend time with Maria and the girls yesterday. Sounds like they had a good time."

"They did. She really likes Lil and Gracie."

"Excuse me." Tristan tipped his hat and went into the barn.

"I should've called you before coming out."

"Perfect timing." I watched her watch Tristan

walk away.

Sarah glanced toward the barn. "I might as well check on Gypsy while I'm here. I'll be out in a bit. By the look on Emma's face, it's gonna be a good day."

Emma's knees peeked through the holes in her faded, distressed denim. She wore a plaid button-down and a straw cowboy hat I suspected belonged to her mother.

Huckleberry poked me with her snout.

"Sorry, Charlie, I fed the sugar to Casanova."

Emma climbed the fence and sat on the upper rail.

"Thanks for playing with the girls yesterday. They had a good time," I told her.

Emma smiled, then pushed the cowboy hat away from her eyes.

"I like the feather in your hat. I like birds."

"Me, too," she said.

"I believe they bring us messages." There were no birds in sight.

Emma inspected the toes of her scuffed cowboy boots.

"Horses are special. I think they understand me more than people. Huck loves the hugs."

"Me, too," Emma whispered.

"Would you like to ride her today?"

Emma nodded.

"She'd like a good brushing before you do."

Emma straddled the fence, then hopped down.

"Come on." I gestured for her to follow me into the barn.

Emma found a brush and a frog pick in the tack room.

"Is it okay if Emma rides Huck?" I asked Sarah.

"Sure is." Sarah stroked Gypsy's rear end.

"How's my girl?"

"Won't know for a while. Looks like she's got a bunkmate though."

"That would be me. I don't want her to be alone." I wished I'd put the cot away.

"Chloe—" Sarah came out of the stall and latched the door.

"I know. I should be sleeping in my own bed." I took a halter from a hook on the wall.

Emma and I went outside. She unlatched the gate and gestured for me to join her. She and I went into the pasture. I slipped the halter over Huck's head and walked her around the pond.

Emma skipped through the field, stopped long enough to pluck a daisy and tuck it in the band of her hat with the hawk's feather. Huck and I met her beneath the shade tree. I picked Huck's feet clean while Emma brushed her.

"Look who's decided not to be stubborn today," I said.

"I can be stubborn, too." Emma patted Huck.

"Good to know. And we can't ride without a saddle." I radioed Tristan. "Could you please bring Huck a saddle? We've got a rider out here."

My dad strode out of the barn with Tristan and Sarah. I held my dad's gaze as he neared. He waited at the fence watching on. Emma climbed the mounting block, swapped her cowboy hat for a helmet, then waited for her cue.

After adjusting the bridle, Tristan and Sarah walked Huckleberry around the perimeter of the field, then Emma rode by herself with confidence. Tristan and Sarah stayed close, chatting about the wildest horses they'd known and the rodeo.

I met Dad at the fence.

"Your head looks like it smarts." I inspected the butterfly strips.

"Looks worse than it is. Didn't sleep so well with Maggie waking me up every few hours."

"She wants to make sure you're okay. She loves you."

"Emma looks like someone I used to know." Dad scratched his whiskers. "Lil and Gracie will be riding before we know it. Time flies."

"Hey, kid." Trout strolled over. "Mr. Featherstone would like to see you."

"You wanna come with me, Dad?"

"I'll be there in a bit. And Chloe—you're doing a great job weeding out the horses. I appreciate your hard work."

"And by the way, Emma wanted to ride. I know where you stand. If you watch long enough though, the bug will get ya. We've got the land. The animals. And the facilities. Not to mention me to oversee the project. It won't be a hobby."

CHAPTER 17

GRAVEL CRUNCHED BENEATH my boot soles— each step heavier than the previous. My walk grew confident as I envisioned a program I wanted to spearhead. I excelled at being the ranch's foreman, and it was time for an additional role. Expanding the family legacy was at the forefront of my mind, a project meant for healing, a program to teach the girls about community awareness and human development.

Lola bolted through the barn doors and ran circles around me.

"That's right, Lola. Bring her in." Justin poked his head from the old barn.

"Ha, ha." His infectious smile lifted what weighed me down. "Dang. You should be worrying about those cattle, not *little old me.*"

"That's not what I hear." He raised a brow.

"Nothing is private. What did Matt tell you?"

"Gosh, nothing. I didn't mean to hit a nerve. It was just a joke."

"Why aren't you out in the field with my dad?"

"Because he asked me to help Mr. Feather-stone. Your daddy seems anxious to finish the barn."

"And I never turn down an extra pair of willing hands, especially if we can finish ahead of schedule," Mr. Featherstone said, joining us.

Justin's dimples showed. He was proud to work. He never needed poking or prodding like the cattle.

"Morning, Chloe." Mr. Featherstone raised his coffee cup.

"Morning, Mr. Featherstone. How's it going?"

"I'm well. We're making good progress. The light fixtures you chose came in. Randy's got an in with the ceiling fans, so we won't have to order them. We'll refinish the floor last. We've got all the new hardware. The trough sink came. Once we install that and the toilets, it'll be functional. Your mom's got great taste." Mr. Featherstone gestured to Justin to follow him. "I'll show you what needs to be done."

"I can work miracles. Jack-of-all-trades." Justin showcased his hands.

"I knew you were more than a handsome face." I patted him on the shoulder.

The scent of fresh timbers washed over me as we stepped inside. The refurbished stalls were finished. "Looks great. These new 'old' doors are perfect."

"Randy found them at Antique Annie's. That woman's got *everything*, and she's ready to haggle." He pointed to the far end of the barn. "I've configured some extra storage for you down there. That didn't take long. We used refurbished planks to finish the bathroom walls."

"This embossed bronzed door handle is fabulous."

"Antique Annie." Mr. Featherstone sipped his coffee.

We made our way upstairs. Bare bulbs hung from the ceiling. The glow from portable, high-wattage lamps lit every nook and cranny.

"We'll install the fixtures before we do the floor. Punching out those four skylights was a piece of cake." He pointed overhead.

"It's coming together." Imagining an intimate group of couples dancing beneath the stars gave me goose bumps. Slow-moving fans throwing light across love-struck partygoers excited me. Red and Bradley would have the perfect wedding.

"Check this out," Mr. Featherstone said. "The lights are on a dimmer. Nice feature for ambiance."

"And we'll be able to see the stars. Let me

know when you're ready for that bear skin rug." The hair stood up on the nape of my neck as I thought about my grandparents.

Mr. Featherstone drank the last of his coffee. "I should be getting to work."

"You know where to find me if you need something." I went downstairs and to the other barn to check on Gypsy. Tristan caught me telling her my woes.

"Hey, cowboy."

"What are you up to?" He slapped his gloves against his thigh; the fringe on his chaps shimmied.

"Gonna hook up the horses and take the girls for a wagon ride. You seem mighty happy these days." His smile was brighter than the sun against his silver stamped belt buckle.

"And you seem a little on edge."

"What did Matt tell you?"

"When it comes to matters of the heart, that's between you and Matt. Would you want Red to break a confidence you asked her not to?" Tristan's jaw flexed, his profile rigid. "I believe your girls are waiting for you."

We hooked Butch and Sundance to the wagon in silence, until impulse got the better of me.

"Did you and Vivian fight? Did you ever say things you didn't mean or not say things you should've?"

Tristan's sideways glance accentuated the dip in his brows.

"Sorry, but I gotta believe you have more insight on this love stuff than you let on. Your eyes tell me so."

"I'm sure if Vivian were here, she'd tell you otherwise." Tristan looked away.

"If you had a bridge to sell, I wouldn't buy it."

"Oh, for the love of the Lord."

Justin emerged from the barn. "What are you two debating now?"

"Come on, what did Matt tell you?" I sounded like a girl with a crush begging her bestie for the inside skinny.

"She ain't likely to give up until she takes us down with her." Justin tucked his working gloves in the back pocket of his jeans.

I flicked the rim of Tristan's cowboy hat. He was mighty handsome and stuffed his feelings deeper than I ever could. "I know something 'bout burying stuff, too."

"It's not my place. Sorry." Tristan fixed his hat.

I spun on a heel and smacked right into Matt.

"Hi, Chloe. Interesting conversation."

Justin and Tristan excused themselves.

"Hi. What's going on?" My cheeks smoldered.

"Branch just called."

"Have you changed your mind?" I didn't want Matt to leave. The words had come out easily, but the feelings not so much.

"It's a great offer, Chloe." Matt planted his hands on his hips. "The calves I want are part of the deal. Like I said before, I need to go."

I went numb. "Does Dad know?"

"Your dad says he understands." Matt shifted his weight with a heavy sigh.

My voice was barely audible. "You can't be serious. Is this because I mentioned a prenup? It was just an idea. Lots of couples have them."

"We're not lots of couples. The girls are waiting for you. We'll talk later."

"You said we'd talk last night, too, but we ended up arguing."

"Last night didn't go like either of us wanted. I'm sorry. There are things here you don't understand."

"I'm sorry, too, and I do understand." Pressing my eyes shut, I saw him walking away, and I couldn't let him. I couldn't spend the rest of my life watching him leave. There'd be plenty of those times ahead with the girls. Worse yet, what if one day he walked away forever? I dropped to one knee and clasped my hands against my heart.

"Marry me." Nervous knots tightened in my belly as the words slipped out. Matt took my hands in his and pulled me to my feet. "Please. Marry me. Don't go to Wyoming."

"Chloe," Matt said with a pleading gaze.

"What? You said you wanted to get married."

"Not like this. Not out of desperation or unreasonable impulse. You deserve so much more—and so do I."

"Let's just do it." I held his doubting gaze. "Plenty of people get married on the spur of the moment."

"Chloe—" Matt's tone was curt. "I wanted to do the proposing. If there was one time I thought you might loosen the reins, I hoped it'd be with this. And this whim for a prenup is proof it's not our time. I'll do what's best for the girls, for us. I wouldn't have it any other way."

The tone of his voice cut me. His response was a hard no. With his chin to the ground, he kicked the fence post, then stormed off.

I'd expected to face the future alone since childhood—I just thought it wouldn't have come so soon.

CHAPTER 18

B EFORE HEADING BACK to the main house, I
went into the barn to speak to Tristan.

"Where'd you go?" I called.

Gypsy stuck her nose over the stall door. I went
into the tack room, grabbed a carrot, and snapped
it into pieces, pretending it was Tristan's body. If it
weren't for him, Branch wouldn't even be in the
picture.

"Where is he?" I fed Gypsy the treat.

Tristan came in from the corral.

"What did you do? Meddler. Branch is your
friend." I poked him in the shoulder.

"Quit poking me." Tristan took me by the
hand. "I didn't do anything."

"Matt's gonna work for Branch."

"I think we're done here. Your dad's expecting
me in the north pasture."

"Traitor," I said.

"There's no need for name-calling. Before you
go blaming me for anything, you should talk to
Matt." Tristan went outside to check the wagon.

"I did. But I think you already know that." Climbing up to the driver's seat, I released the brake and snapped the reins. "Let's go, you two."

Tristan shrugged. His gaze followed the wagon as I pulled out. Matt came around the barn. They stood side by side, the man I'd trusted and the man I'd learned to respect. How could Matt leave the ranch? How could he tell me he wouldn't marry me? After all, that's what he wanted.

I stopped the wagon at the main house. Maggie helped Lil down the front steps, and Red assisted Gracie. Glad shut the front door behind her, and the posse of women climbed into the wagon bed.

"Isn't anyone going to ride up here with me?" I asked.

"Sure will, cowboy," Glad said with a nod of her head. "I'll need a hand though."

I hopped down from the driver's seat and ran around to the other side of the wagon to help her.

"I knew you'd have my back," she said.

Her sentiment hung in the air. I'd need someone to say those words to me if Matt wouldn't be around.

"Thanks for helping Mom," Maggie said.

"She's been bugging me all morning to ask for help if I need it. Enough with the overprotectiveness, Maggie Jean." Glad tsked.

"Hips don't always mend, Mom."

"What's with the hips, Maggie? A hip is better than a heart." Glad patted my hand. "Can I drive?"

"Maybe on the way back." I returned to the driver's seat.

"I've heard *that* before," Glad sputtered.

Maggie and Red situated the girls. Lil's belly laugh made me smile. Gracie wiggled into the corner behind me, crossed her legs, and put her hands in her lap.

"You gals ready back there?" I waited.

Maggie wrapped her arms around Lil, and Red gave me the high sign. I released the brake, clicked my tongue, then snapped the reins. Butch and Sundance took us down the dusty road toward the river. The strain in my jaw ached as I thought about Matt. He'd really turned down my proposal.

"What's gotten into you, Chloe?" Glad said over the sound of horse hooves.

"Nothing." I kept my thoughts to myself, but I wasn't sure why. Maggie and Dad lived day to day as a couple, and Glad—she'd mastered the art of living with and without her husband. Bradley and Red had their lives in order. Me, I'd managed to evade marriage and divorce successfully at the expense of a relationship I took for granted.

"You look upset," Glad said.

"Why would I be upset?" I stopped the horses near the river. Jumping down from my seat, I didn't give my riders a second thought. I kicked at the ground and grumbled.

"What in heaven's name has gotten into you?" Maggie unlatched the back door of the wagon. Golden flecks in her hazel irises shimmered in the sunshine.

"What does he think he's doing? He can go for all I care," I spouted like a hot kettle. Trouble was, I cared.

Maggie covered Lil's ears. "She'll repeat every word you say."

"I doubt it. She's sweet as pie."

"Eventually, she will. Trust me."

"Can someone get me down from here? All this talk about hips has got me a little nervous," Glad called through cupped hands.

"I'm coming." Maggie hurried to help her mom.

Red unloaded the wagon. Lil and Gracie toddled along, sniffing wildflowers. Red followed behind, picking enough for a bouquet. When Glad was steady on solid ground, Maggie took me by the arm.

"What?" I shook my head. "I'm sorry. I

shouldn't be snippy with you."

She was everything lovely, wise, and I wished I had one-tenth of her demeanor. She squeezed my hand and didn't let go.

"You haven't exactly been yourself lately," she said.

"You're telling me. I'm no good at trying to pretend."

"Most people aren't."

"Why do relationships have to be so hard?" I squatted at the river's edge, picked up a skipping stone, and whipped it into the slow-moving current. Looking up, I studied her face, wondering what it was like to be married to her. "Has Dad done anything so maddening you just wanted to throttle him?"

"We've had our challenges." Maggie kneeled.

"The challenges are wearing me down." Picking up another rock, I tossed it into the river. It sank with a kerplunk. "Life is hard enough with an injured horse who doesn't seem to be making progress, twins, and living with your family." Rattling off three excuses made my belly-aching sound plausible.

"We're really difficult to live with?" Maggie sounded hurt.

"I knew you'd call me out," I said.

Glad, Red, and the girls joined us.

"What's going on? That's a pretty serious face, Chloe." Glad jostled Lil on her hip, then set her down.

"No. No. No!" Lil stood next to Gracie and shook her finger at the river. "No!"

"I have no idea what's got her in a tizzy. She says we're difficult to live with." Maggie planted a hand on her hip. "I know you don't mean that."

"No, I don't." I composed myself. "Can we focus on Matt?"

"We're difficult to live with." Glad scrunched up her face. Lil mimicked her.

"No. No. No!" Lil shook her finger and marched back and forth.

"I shouldn't have said that." I regretted my words.

"I can't imagine anyone I'd rather live with." Red sat next to Gracie.

Gracie played with the ends of Red's hair, rubbing the fine strands between her tiny fingers.

"Me either." I plopped down next to Red. "I'm just upset. Haven't you ever said anything you didn't mean?" My words came out in an exasperated jumble. "Things *are not* going my way."

"Apparently," Maggie said.

"Before we get sidetracked again, can I see a

show of hands of those who know about Matt's job offer in Wyoming?" I groaned when Maggie and Glad exchanged glances. "I figured."

Red shook her head. Lil and Gracie held up their arms.

Maggie helped Glad to the ground, then Lil crawled into her lap.

"Freaking Wyoming. We live in Montana. He has no idea what he's leaving behind." I tucked loose strands of hair behind my ears.

"Oh, I think he does," Glad said.

"Dang it," Gracie mimicked.

Maggie and Glad both stared at me with *I told you so* expressions. "Yeah, yeah, yeah. I know." I held my arms out to Gracie, and she fell into them. "I shouldn't say those words. I'm sorry." I took in Red's frown. "Poor timing on my part. And Red, Matt's taking a job in Wyoming."

"Seems to me if you let things play out naturally, maybe you'd feel differently." Maggie sat next to her mom.

"Loving someone isn't just sleeping next to each other night after night," Glad said.

"Or asking them to marry you because you thought it would make him want to stay." I buried my face in the palms of my hands. "And I mentioned having a prenup. You know, to have a safety net while we're both thinking straight."

"You didn't," Maggie said.

"I did. And let's just say that didn't make things better."

Gracie stroked my cheek. Her eyes appeared to understand more than I thought she was capable of. I sold everyone short, including myself.

Kicking at the grass, I walked away with heavy legs and an even heavier heart. I bent down, picked up a handful of pebbles from the riverbank, and tossed them into the river one by one. The clasp of my necklace pulled the hair at the nape of my neck. I threw the rest of the rocks into the water. I tugged at the strands of tangled hair, then undid the clasp. I caressed the silver heart necklace my mother had given me when I was a young girl, stroking the worn metal, and prayed that Matt and I would work things out.

A gust of wind blew my cowboy hat over my eyes, and my feet slipped out from underneath me. My most cherished possession fell into the rambling water. I fumbled on the rocky riverbed, trying to catch it. In the blink of an eye, my necklace was gone.

CHAPTER 19

FTER DROPPING THE girls, Maggie, Glad, and Red off at the main house, I drove the wagon back to the barn. Trout stood near the adjacent pasture, smoking a cigarette, the curve in his upper lip as if he knew I was coming. I parked the wagon and jumped down from the driver's seat.

"What in tarnation happened to you?" Trout took a long drag from his cigarette.

I scowled, took the radio from my belt, then called Justin to come help with the horses.

"You're wetter than a tomcat in a hailstorm." Trout snubbed out his smoke and tucked the butt in the red box he carried in his shirt pocket.

"Surlier than one, too." I refused to give in to the sting behind my eyes. I stomped into the barn and tossed my hat on the tack box. I pulled the wet bandanna from my damp pocket, tied it around my head, and avoided Trout's stare. The silence was louder than the morning run with the horses.

Gypsy poked her head over the stall door. Her whiskers twitched as she sniffed me. I stroked her velvety nose. She completely, undeniably under-stood me. No words were needed. Gypsy pushed her nose into the palm of my hand. I attempted to retrieve sugar cubes from my pocket, but they had dissolved from the knee-deep water my jeans soaked up. "Sorry, girl. I don't have anything." I fingered her mane.

"Gypsy seems to be holding her own," Trout said.

"Not exactly the recovery I had in mind. Was Sarah here today?"

"Not yet." Trout offered me a smoke, the curl in his upper lip returning.

I stared at him.

"Gosh, must be bad if I can't get a rise out of you." Trout put the cigarette box back in his shirt pocket. "Why are you soaked?"

"I lost my necklace in the river, and I went in after it." I touched my neck—would I ever get used to not wearing it?

"You would've kicked yourself for not trying to save what you love."

"Maybe I'll have a smoke after all." Water squished through my toes. I rested my head against Gypsy.

"Must be bad." Deep valleys lined his fore-head.

"Yeah, it's bad."

"Sorry, kid."

"Yeah, me, too."

Sarah and Tristan walked through the barn door. Tristan was telling Sarah the story of how he acquired Casanova.

"Well, look what the cat dragged in. What in the world happened to you?" Tristan eyed me from head to toe.

Trout shook his head at him.

"Are you okay?" Sarah asked.

"I went into the river."

"On purpose," Tristan said.

"Yes, *on purpose*. I lost my favorite necklace." Gypsy nudged my shoulder, her breath warm against my neck.

"I think we've all had those days," Sarah said.

She didn't have a clue what had transpired between Matt and me. I chose to dismiss the comment and moved out of the way of the stall door. I tucked my fingers into my pocket, feeling for the miniature lucky horseshoe Matt had given me. I couldn't find it. I walked outside, kicked the fencepost, and swore under my breath.

"When you're done with the tantrum, Sarah would like to talk to you." Trout squeezed my shoulder and went back inside the barn.

My hands shook. Tucking them in my back pockets didn't temper the nerves.

"There don't seem to be any significant changes." Sarah ran her hand down Gypsy's leg.

"I've done everything I'm supposed to."

"I know this is hard. Only time will tell. Patience can sometimes be the best medicine."

"She has to get better." My gaze met Trout's. "Where's Emma?"

"At the main house with Maggie and the girls." Sarah's gaze caught Tristan's. "Let me see that leg one last time, girl." Gypsy picked up her hoof on cue. I glanced at Tristan, then at Trout, who hadn't taken his eyes off me.

Sarah produced a few bits of carrot from her pocket.

"Looks like Chloe isn't the only one bribing the livestock around here," Tristan said, tapping me on the shoulder.

I buried my face in my girl's neck and hugged her.

"Keep doing what you're doing," Sarah said. "Such a pretty girl."

"She's the best," I said, appreciating her strength and loyalty. Tristan peered at me from the corner of his eyes. When his gaze met Sarah's, his dark eyes sparkled. He was moving on, and I needed to as well.

"I appreciate all the time you've spent checking on Gypsy. Thank you."

"You're welcome," she replied, latching the stall door. "We'll adjust her regimen if we need to."

I shook Sarah's hand and left the barn. Back home, I kicked my dirt-caked boots off at the mudroom door and peeled off my socks. I undid my belt, pulled my damp shirt away from my skin, and called Maggie on the kitchen landline.

"Hi, Chloe." Laughter filled the background.

"What's going on there?"

"Bradley flew in today."

"Thought he was coming next week."

"Total surprise. The best kind."

"I'll be over in a bit to get the girls."

"They're not here. Glad's at your place now with them."

"They must be upstairs. Thanks."

Feeling sorry for myself, I trudged upstairs. I had some apologies to make after cleaning myself up. This place wouldn't be the same without Matt. I stood on the landing at the top of the stairs, listening to the soft murmurs coming from the girls' room.

When I peeked in on them, Glad was passed

out on the floor. I dropped to my knees and felt for a pulse. The girls had curled up against her, sucking their thumbs and holding vigil like a couple of pups. I grabbed the landline in the hallway and dialed the main house, then used my two-way radio to alert the others.

"Get over here. Now. Glad's collapsed. Get Dad. Call for help. She's got a heartbeat. Just get here!" I hung up and ran back to the bedroom. Kneeling next to her, I said a prayer while stroking her hand. Her limp fingers were cold. My shoulders quaked. Gracie frowned.

"I'm sorry, baby girl. I'm sorry. Momma doesn't mean to upset you."

Footsteps echoed in the hallway. I wiped my eyes with the bottom of my shirt. Glancing over my shoulder, I yelled, "We're in here."

Maggie stopped in the doorway, gripping the doorframe.

"What do we do? Where's Dad?"

Sarah came running into the room with her medical bag.

"Please, Glad, wake up," I begged.

"Mom." Maggie kneeled next to me and caressed her mom's forearm. "Are the girls okay?"

"They're fine." I squeezed Glad's hand.

Sarah pulled a stethoscope from her bag. She

listened to Glad's heart and held her wrist. Tristan entered the crowded room.

The knot at the back of my throat grew. Maggie put her arm around my shoulder. "Tristan, find John, now! Help is on the way!"

Tristan did as he was told.

"Chloe, take the girls downstairs." Maggie's stricken stare glassed over. "Now," she said, her hushed order direct.

She pried my hand from Glad's. Lil touched her hair, and I ushered her and Gracie into the hall.

Tristan ended the call with my dad, then picked up Lil. His shoulders slumped forward as he walked down the eerie hallway. Gracie nuzzled into me, my neck damp from her soft whimpers.

"I know, baby girl. Let's get you downstairs."

In the living room, Tristan set Lil in the over-sized leather chair big enough for a family of four. "You should get out of those wet clothes. I'll wait with the girls."

Gracie clung to me when I tried to set her down.

"Bring her over here." Tristan opened his arms. His dark eyes brimmed with concern.

Letting go was hard, but I did. Bradley and Red rushed in from the kitchen.

"She's upstairs with Maggie and Sarah." I led

the way. Their voices drifted into the hallway. I peeked into the twins' room. Glad had opened her eyes, her hand on her forehead.

"Mom. Lie still." Maggie caressed her mother's hair.

Dad rushed into the room. His *this doesn't look good* expression unnerved me. Swallowing hard, I forced myself to move. He settled in next to Maggie and Sarah on the floor. Bowing my head, I closed my eyes, wondering how to bargain with God. Matt's voice brushed my ear.

"You're soaked," he said, squeezing my shoulder.

"I know." I rushed to the window. The air ambulance hovered above the empty pasture, the whir of the engine muffled by the glass. First Matt, now Glad. I reached for my necklace I'd clung to when I needed strength, and it wasn't there.

"Go get changed." Matt tugged at my hand. "Now. Bradley and Red are with the girls."

"The air ambulance is here. I'll show them up," Tristan called from downstairs.

I closed my bedroom door, peeled off my pants, and left them in a crumpled heap on the floor. I wiggled out of my panties and shirt. I caught a glimpse of myself in the mirror hanging above the dresser. My face was smudged with mud. Straggly wisps of hair fell over my shoulders.

Take me. Spare Glad. Maggie needs her. It's not her time.

A soft knock took me from my thoughts while I rummaged for clean clothing. Matt came in with a warm washcloth and clean towel. He'd seen me naked plenty of times, but this time felt different.

"Thought you might need some help."

I wiped my body with the washcloth, then dried off. I'd shower later. I put on a clean bra and panties, then sat at the end of the bed, listening hard to the muffled voices in the adjoining room. Matt tugged a tee over my head, and I pushed my arms through the armholes. "Why now?"

"Get dressed, Chloe. We need your help."

He was right. Crumbling now wouldn't do any good. I put on the fresh pair of jeans without looking away from the man who was on the threshold of leaving, too.

"Glad's tough," he said.

"We don't even know what happened." I pointed to a dry pair of boots in the corner. He grabbed them and put them on my feet.

"Whatever it is, she'll fight. She always does." His lips were warm against my ear. "Finish cleaning up. I'll be downstairs."

I studied the sad eyes staring back at me in the

mirror hanging above the dresser. I brushed my hair, tied one of my grandmother's bandannas around my head, and said another prayer.

I opened the bedroom door. Dad, Sarah, and Maggie huddled in the hallway. I peeked over them to where the paramedics worked. Glad's petite frame was as limp as wet sheets when they lifted her. The snap of the buckles sent a chill up my spine. The rachet of the gurney a sound I'd heard only on television.

We moved from the path, then followed the paramedics and Glad downstairs.

"I'm going with her," Maggie insisted.

"We'll be there as soon as we can." Dad kissed her taut temple.

Helplessness evoked fear as I stood in the shadows. How many holes could an individual withstand? Too many would surely result in collapse.

CHAPTER 20

G LAD APPEARED GAUNT and fragile, her skin a whiter shade of pale. Her petite body was swallowed by a pastel checked hospital gown and white linens. Dad stood beside her bed, put his arm around my shoulder, and I held onto him.

"Why don't you sit with her for a bit? Bradley took Maggie to get some coffee."

Saline dripped through the IV, and lights blipped across a screen displaying her vitals. The blue vinyl chair was unforgiving against my body. Dad left the room.

The three of us sat in silence. Glad. Me. And God. I held Glad's hand. She loved me. Scolded me. Inspired me. Guided me. And I loved her more than she'd ever know.

Her plaid printed reading glasses were on the nightstand. She had said the plaid was the same colors as the family tartan of her Scottish relatives. I put them on, balanced them on the end of my nose, and peered through the lenses. They blurred my vision.

"You should be wearing these. There isn't a day I don't remember you peering over the rim of your glasses, and boy, do you have a lot of them. You could give that guy who sings about a yellow brick road a run for his money. I can't remember his name, but that's understandable because I've only got one thing on my mind, and that's taking you home."

I wrapped my fingers around hers and held tight. I'd done a fine job of collecting people in my lifetime, and Glad was a gem. "Please don't take her. She's not done here." I bowed my head in prayer.

Glad tugged my hand. She'd heard me, knew I was here, and peeked through narrow slits.

"I'm tired," she said.

"It's okay, Gladiola. Just rest. I won't leave."

"I know." She closed her eyes, then opened them again. "I saw angels."

Leaning closer, I held her green stare. Regardless of my wishes, I knew there wasn't any bargaining with angels. They were the messengers, the ones watching over us. "What did they look like?"

"They're extremely tall. Bigger than this room. Can you see them?"

I looked around the drab room, not able to see

what she described. "The only angel I see is you."

"They showed me the light."

Bradley returned and sat on the other side of the bed. His jaw clenched. His temple pulsated. He studied the machines, then kissed the back of his nana's hand.

Glad laid still, her gaze fixated on him. Memories of saying goodbye to Grandpa Winston flooded back. Was he one of the angels Glad had seen? Closing my eyes, I rested my head on the edge of the bed. If she hadn't been tethered to wires and tubing, I would've crawled beneath the covers with her.

"Chloe," Bradley said. "The doctor's here."

I sat up. Gray whiskers dotted his chin. Dad and Maggie stood at the foot of Glad's bed.

"I'm Dr. Hodges. I've gone over Glad's tests." He skimmed the notes on the medical chart. "She's suffered a heart attack. We'll monitor her over the next forty-eight hours. Her blood pressure is low. We'll keep a close eye on her vitals and make sure she's comfortable. Oxygen level is 95 percent."

Maggie's teary stare met Bradley's gaze. Dad shook Dr. Hodges's hand and asked if he could have a moment in the hallway. Maggie joined them.

Bradley and I stayed with Glad. Monitors

beeped, and Glad nodded off.

"She's tough," Bradley said. "With rest and rehab, she'll recover."

Glad opened her eyes.

"Winston sends his best, dear girl. And Bradley, your grandfather is handsome as ever."

"She's still got a sense of humor." But making light of the moment didn't ease my heavy heart.

The corner of Bradley's mouth lifted. "How do you feel?"

"Okay. Nothing hurts. I'm ready to go home though. This gown is for the birds."

"Your color is coming back." I stroked her cheek. "They're going to keep an eye on you." A chill shimmied down my spine.

"Can you turn on the light over my bed? It's getting dark outside. Can I have my glasses? I feel naked without them."

I handed her the glasses, and Bradley switched on the reading lamp attached to the bed.

"It's better in the light," she said.

Maggie and Dad returned. "We should let her rest," Dad said. "How about we get a bite to eat, then come up and tuck her in."

"It's going to be a long night. Probably should call Matt and Red and let them know what's going on."

"I'll be back. Don't you go anywhere." I kissed Glad's forehead.

"You got it, kiddo." Glad adjusted the oxygen tube. "These tubes are a nuisance."

"I know," Maggie said, smoothing her mom's hair back. "Necessary precautions aren't always practical."

"Where are my knitting needles? I'm gonna need something to do while I'm here."

"They're at home, Mom. Someone will bring them tomorrow."

"Let's give Maggie and Bradley a minute." Dad took me by the hand and led me into the hallway. Dr. Hodges stood reviewing charts at the nurse's station. The metallic hospital smell and aroma of disinfectant tickled my nose. Florescent lighting cast a strange unnatural hue over the area, and everything seemed cold.

Bradley joined us, buried his hands in his pockets, and paced. His gaze focused on the floor. Then Maggie came out, took a deep breath, clasped her hands to her chest, and closed her eyes for a brief moment.

"We'll be in the cafeteria," Dad told the nurses.

Dr. Hodges handed Maggie a tissue, and she dried her cheeks.

"Thank you for being prepared with your

mom's legal documents. I know this is difficult," he said. "From what I see in her chart and her health history, the odds are in her favor. I'll be here tonight if you have any questions." He checked his phone and nodded with a reassuring smile.

"Thank you." Maggie returned to Glad's room.

We watched through the window. Maggie kissed her mom's forehead, then sat next to her on the bed. Glad shooed her away with a giggle, making Maggie smile.

Maggie blew Gladiola another kiss from the doorway, then we made our way down the hall to the elevator. The shiny doors opened. But before we could board, an alarm went off, and someone yelled Gladiola's name. The nurses and Dr. Hodges scrambled into her room.

Bradley and I ran back, too, and huddled together, watching through the window. Maggie sobbed in Dad's embrace. Bradley held my hand.

The heart monitor flatlined.

"She doesn't want to be resuscitated." Bradley's voice trembled.

"No!" I gripped the cool steel window frame. "It's not her time."

CHAPTER 21

FIVE DAYS HAD come and gone since we lost Glad. Maggie had written a loving obituary and organized what seemed like hundreds of archived photos, sat for hours sipping tea, talking to Gladiola like she'd never died.

The sun pushed away the heavy darkness lying on the horizon. She'd been here, and in a blink of an eye, she'd vanished. Glad had been called home. I reached for the silver heart hanging from my necklace until I remembered it had been washed downriver. I bowed my head and wept.

Bradley handed me a box of tissues and sat beside me in the grass. I leaned my head against his burly shoulder.

"This sucks," I said.

"I'd thought she'd live forever." Bradley yanked a scraggly piece of grass from the dewy ground. "Our butts are going to be wet. You know that, don't you?"

"I don't care."

"Me neither." Bradley took in a sharp breath.

"Mom's finalizing the list of things that need to be done. Including taking Nana's ashes to Michigan." She was to be buried with her husband at the Shady Oaks Cemetery in Grosse Pointe after a short service. "I haven't been back to Michigan in years, not even to see my dad. He usually comes to Boston." His sigh was monumental. "It'll be just us at the cemetery."

We huddled together like lost children. Sad. Defeated. Heartbroken.

"It's not fair," I said.

Bradley squared his shoulders. "We both know life's not fair, and I don't think we're supposed to keep score. Keeping score takes the fun out of it." He pointed to the frayed clouds overhead. "Angel wings."

"Bigger than life. Like our Gladiola." I pulled grass from the ground, roots and all. Bradley took the accidental clump from me, placed the roots back into the hole I hadn't meant to make, and replanted it.

"I'm glad you'll be here for my mom," he said. "I'm not sure you'll ever understand how grateful I am that she has you. I always felt bad for not being there when she and my dad got divorced. When you showed up, you helped fill the void."

"It's not a big deal. You couldn't help it. You

had school, a whole life ahead of you, and things to accomplish in Boston."

"It *is* a big deal. Because of you, I felt a whole lot less guilty about living my life. I knew once you'd gotten under her skin, she'd never want to let you go. She was like that with the children she taught. Your presence gave her purpose."

"You're welcome. My dad was a bonus." I smiled through the tears.

The mountains came alive in the budding light. I pictured Glad tugging at the blanket of night, exposing the brilliant sunrise. Matt, Tristan, Justin, and Quinn rode across the way, rounded up the horses in the distance, and ran them home. The thunderous hooves against the earth didn't drown out the loss of our Gladiola.

"Chloe?"

"Yeah, Bradley."

"She wouldn't want us to be sad. She'd want you to be bringing the horses home. She'd want you to take her with you wherever you go."

"I know. With Gypsy out of commission, it makes it easier to sit on the sidelines."

"Will you promise me you'll ride tomorrow morning?"

"Yes." I zipped my Sherpa fleece to my chin.

Red strolled across the field. "Do you mind if I

join you?"

"Got a damp seat right here." Bradley patted the ground.

"I came prepared. Would you like to share?" She unfolded a plaid blanket.

Bradley stood, took me by the hands, and got me to my feet while Red placed the blanket where we had been sitting.

"Thank you for helping Maria feed the girls breakfast." I sat back down, stretched out my legs, and leaned back on bent elbows.

"They both went back to sleep after they ate." Red sat next to Bradley and rested her head on his shoulder. "It's so beautiful here. Even in the sadness."

"I'll leave you alone to enjoy the scenery. You'll be back in Boston the day after tomorrow." I stood, stretched my legs, left the lovebirds alone, and went inside. I sipped coffee and stared out the kitchen window. Love didn't stop because of hurt. Love didn't evaporate into the void created from loss. Love couldn't be measured. Love was endless, like the blue Montana sky. I'd just have to learn to love Glad from afar like I did Grandpa and Ida May. I'd have to watch and most importantly, listen. Glad would find a way to be with me. She'd find a way to be with all of us. I set my empty coffee cup in the sink.

She already had.

MAGGIE HAD PLANNED every aspect of our trip back to Michigan before Bradley and Red had flown back to Boston and gone back to work. Bradley had called me every night for a week at nine o'clock to check in after talking to Maggie. He reassured me he and Red would pick us up at the airport in Detroit. This life-altering event had brought us closer, and I wondered if our support for each other had been part of Glad's plan all along.

The plane touched down with a bumpy screech, halting my daydreams. The dreary Michigan landscape appeared out the tiny window I pressed my nose against like a child taking in the tarmac full of planes, thinking about Lil and Gracie back home.

Maggie clutched the leather backpack holding Glad's ashes in the airline-approved container. Maggie had chosen a wooden box embossed with Celtic filigree.

"I can't believe we're here," I said. "I didn't think I'd ever see this place again."

"I'd like to get off the plane now," Maggie said

as the plane crawled toward the gate. "This is torture."

"I know," Dad said, patting her hand.

When the seat belt sign went off, Maggie shot out of her seat, crawled over my dad, and opened the overhead bin. Dad stood, took her hand, and whispered something in her ear. She took a deep breath and let him get our carry-ons. I turned on my phone to check for messages. The only one was from Bradley. He'd sent a photo of the car he rented and a short note. I had hoped there'd be something from Maria or Matt.

Maria had offered to stay later in the evenings to help Matt with the girls. Sarah had also volunteered to help out. Our heart-to-heart eased my conscience about leaving Lil and Gracie. She'd reminded me how she'd raised Emma alone, and reassured me the girls would be fine.

Quite the opposite of my relationship with Matt, but in my fear, I'd nudged him out the door. I'd used Red and Bradley's wedding as an excuse to dodge Matt's intentions—and needs, a diversion of denial that achieved nothing. Then I'd focused on the therapy center, sent out a grant and not told anyone in hopes of gaining a tangible positive. Matt and I hadn't had the discussion we'd avoided or that I needed. Losing Glad was the granddaddy of smokescreens keeping us cordial. Matt had helped me pack, let me sob on his shoulder, and promised he'd be there for the girls while I was out of town.

Glad was gone, and I was in Michigan with Dad and Maggie to bury her ashes when the only place I wanted to be was back home with the girls and Matt.

Dad checked his phone messages while we waited on the curb, breathing in exhaust and chaotic airport energy.

"I sure don't miss this place," he said.

"Neither do I." I covered my nose when a rusted-out sedan drove past and left a trail of fumes. "There's Bradley." I waved him over and helped Dad load the bags in the back of the sedan. "Red's at his dad's house."

Maggie got in the passenger's seat, and Dad belted her in. She stared straight ahead and hugged Glad's ashes.

The forty-minute drive to Grosse Pointe took us through urban neighborhoods, defunct buildings, factories, and graffitied landscape until we came to the quaint communities with pristine lawns and gardens. The drive along the lake brought back memories, picnics with Glad, visits with my mom, and long days playing. We passed the park with the little sandy beach and made a left on the road where Maggie's stone house and our brick colonial house shared a narrow strip of grass and privacy fence.

Bradley slowed in front of his childhood home. Three young girls played hopscotch in the drive. Sidewalk chalk littered the ground. One little girl with long tangled blonde hair blew bubbles from a bubble wand while dancing in bare feet. She tripped over the pile of shoes in the grass and landed on her bottom. She spilled her bubbles and laughed. I rolled down the window.

"It looks the same," I said. "It feels strange being here."

"Sure does," said Bradley. "It's like I never lived here."

"This is harder than I imagined." Maggie's voice trailed off.

"If Dad hadn't purchased the house next door, we might've never met," I said.

"That would've been a shame," Maggie said. "I wonder if my tomato garden is still there."

The three girls stopped playing and stared back at us. Bradley waved, and we drove on.

"I'll head back to Dad's after I drop you off at the Goldsterns'." Bradley stopped at the corner. "I can see Nana's house from here."

Maggie rolled down her window and asked Bradley to turn the corner. Bradley put on his blinker and made a right.

"I bet your dad's excited to see you," I said, trying to break the lull of sadness.

Bradley parked the car in front of Maggie's childhood home, the house where Glad had lived before moving to the 617 Ranch. The shades were drawn. The flowers were sparse, and the once-orange mailbox was now a drab brown.

"It was a much happier house when Nana lived here."

"The Goldsterns are waiting for us. Goodbye, house. Goodbye, Mom." Maggie rolled up her window and rested her forehead on the glass. "This is some memory lane."

The remaining five-minute car ride was spent in silence. Mr. and Mrs. Goldstern waited on the porch.

"It's nice of them to let us stay with them," I said.

Bradley parked in the drive. Maggie was met with open arms. She and Mrs. Goldstern had been friends for as long as I could remember. I'd played with her sons, Harry and Walter, when I lived here. We were the best of friends.

Bradley excused himself after taking the bags inside.

"We'll see you later. I'm looking forward to meeting Red," Mrs. Goldstern said.

I peered through the green canopy overhead. Blue patches peeked through the swaying branches of massive oak trees.

"Everything feels off," I said.

"It most certainly does." Maggie hugged her backpack to her chest.

"At least we have each other."

CHAPTER 22

MAGGIE WORE A black sleeveless dress with embroidered flowers above the hem in bold garden colors, patent leather flats, and a black cardigan with pockets to hold her tissue. I stood next to Bradley in a new black eyelet skirt and a cropped black linen jacket I'd paired with a white blouse and the studded boots my mom had given me. The vestibule of the Presbyterian church decorated with photos of Glad and vases of gladiolas didn't make this day any easier.

People filed in. Bradley and Maggie greeted them with smiles and pleasant conversation. Dad and Red handed out bulletins, while I tried to be invisible.

"This must be Chloe. You're all grown up. I'm Lois. Glad and I were good friends. We played cards together, knitted, and even traveled together before she moved west. I missed her then, and boy, will I miss her now. We had a standing Wednesday night phone call." Lois's silver bob framed her full face.

"It's nice to meet you, Lois. Thanks for being such a good friend," I said.

Maggie took Lois by the hand and led her to a seat near Judy Goldstern and her husband, Pink.

"How are you holding up?" Bradley asked.

"I've been better. What about you, big brother?" The deep breath I took didn't instill the sense of peace I'd hoped for.

He answered with a shrug and buried his hands in his suit pockets. "I don't remember or know most of these folks." He greeted a gentleman with a cane. "Hello."

"I'm Mr. Wallace. I lived down the street from your grandmother. You used to mow my lawn. I recognize the red hair."

Bradley's gaze brightened. "You're Ben. Nice to see you. You used to tip me with a cold root beer. Every time. You were my favorite customer."

"And no one cut my lawn as well as you. It's been a long time. I'll be ninety-three next week." Ben shook Bradley's hand, then made his way down the aisle after looking at the framed photos of Glad on the table.

When the vestibule emptied, a bagpiper wearing traditional Highland dress came in from outside. Glad's request for a Scottish farewell had been made long ago, and Maggie made sure her mother's wish was fulfilled. She and the bagpiper chatted for a moment before we made our way to the front pew where Red waited for us. The bagpiper remained at the rear of the sanctuary, playing "Amazing Grace."

The haunting sound took me to a country I'd never visited. Visions of green quilted mountainsides, abandoned castles on moors, and kilted men came to mind.

Fidgeting with the tissue in hand, I stared at my feet. I counted the studs on the shaft of my right boot, then the left. This was too damn hard.

Maggie spoke after the minister delivered a short sermon and led us in prayer. Bradley read a tribute he had written. His words were eloquent and heartfelt. He'd put his grief aside. Me, I'd pushed it deep down.

Dad put his arm around me. I forced myself to look at him, and when I did, the loss trickled through my body. It stole my breath and made my muscles ache. I pushed my emotions down, again and again until the service ended.

During the moment of silence after the minister's last words, sun pierced the stained glass windows, throwing a rainbow of color across the sanctuary, and for a second I felt *her,* and I knew she'd always be with me.

As we left the church, the bagpiper played a tune called "Mist Covered Mountains." It seemed fitting, a tribute to Glad's roots and the Montana landscape she called home in her final days.

Glad's friends filed out of the church and said their goodbyes. Red and I handed out stalks of vibrant gladiolas to her friends.

After the parking lot emptied, Maggie sobbed and Dad held her. Bradley opened his arms to me. I fell into them, and he consoled me.

MAGGIE CRADLED HER mom's urn and gazed at the headstone her parents shared. Dad brought folding chairs from the trunk of the car and arranged them around the hole in the ground where Glad's ashes would be placed by the end of the day. Bradley, Red, Dad, and I hung back, giving Maggie space. The tune she hummed was unfamiliar. Upon finishing her song, she held a conversation with her mom as if Glad were standing by her side.

I pushed my sunglasses to the top of my head and leaned toward Bradley.

"What do you think they're talking about?"

"If I had to guess, I'd say Nana's doing the talking and Mom's listening." Bradley chuckled.

"That sounds about right." My gaze scanned

the neighboring cemetery plots adorned with flowers, plants, wreaths, statues, and flags. Twelve geese flew overhead in a spectacular vee formation.

"Glad's advice is usually top-notch. Maybe I should get in on the conversation. I could use some of her wisdom." I strained to hear Maggie, but her muffled words were lost in the open space between us. When my hair fluttered against my cheek, I tucked it behind my ear.

"I'll be back in a few minutes." I walked down the narrow pebbly road, reading the gravestones and monuments. I couldn't see the lake, but I could smell it. The fresh scent brought back an earlier time, a time that seemed so far away, almost nonexistent. I listened. My memories weren't the only ones floating in the air.

I focused on Bradley. He was a beacon of good energy. He stood alone and was surrounded by a past I could only imagine. The life I'd known with Gladiola had been unique and special to me in a different way.

Bradley, Maggie, Dad, and I were a family, as tightknit as one of Glad's knitting projects. I wandered back after Maggie set Glad's urn on a small table next to the Abernathy headstone, a vase of gladiolas on each side. When she sat, so did the rest of us.

My thoughts wandered. What were Matt and the girls doing?

The hole in the ground was like a tourist attraction. We discussed the depth, Glad's husband, Walter, the plants and urns on the adjacent plots, Maggie's family history, and stories she'd never shared. Not because she didn't want to, but because she said there was a time and place, and that time and place was now. We laughed. We cried. We consoled each other.

"Can I hold Glad's urn?" I asked.

Bradley took it from the table.

"For a petite woman, she's pretty heavy." He paused. "Who knew?"

"Where do you think she is now?" I asked.

Maggie chuckled. The hem of her black dress fluttered around her shins. "If I had to bet, I'd say she's driving down Lakeshore in a convertible with the top down, wondering what we're doing sitting around this hole, talking about cemetery guidelines, when there's a lake to enjoy and people to see."

Red giggled and kicked off her high heels.

Bradley smiled. "She'll stop at the park and sit on a bench by the shore. I'm sure she's got her knitting bag, a new pair of glasses to celebrate a new beginning, and one of her silk scarves tied around her head." His pointer finger shot up. "Not because she's older, but because it reminds her of the 1950s, her favorite era."

"I'm sure she's not alone. I bet Bones is with her," I said.

"Ah, yes. She's with the most curious dog ever. I bet they're eating ice cream." Maggie nodded. "And I'm sure my father is by her side. He's probably asking her what took so long."

"I'm going to miss her sneaking up on me, her sense of humor, and her cooking. She's made up for the time I missed out with my mother. I'm sure Ida May's introduced herself by now." Dad held Maggie's hand.

Each one of us grieved for a woman we loved. Her importance touched us all in different ways.

"She could fill *holes* better than anyone I knew." I placed the urn back on the table.

"It's nice here," Red said.

"It *is*. We should've brought cocktails." Maggie sighed.

"Margaritas." Bradley gazed into the green canopy overhead.

"I'll miss her something fierce. Tomorrow, I'll wake up only to be reminded she's gone." Maggie dabbed at the corner of her eyes with a tissue.

The cemetery's caretaker strolled toward us, his

hands in his pockets. "You folks doing all right over here?"

"Yes," Dad answered.

"When you're ready to leave, place the urn in the hole. Let me know, and I'll take care of the rest before dark. I'll be in the office if you need anything."

"Thank you." Dad stood and shook his hand.

"I'm sorry for your loss." The caretaker bowed his head, then walked away.

Maggie took an envelope of photos from her purse, skimmed the contents, and set them on the table. Bradley and Red looked at them before handing them to me. I read the writing on the back of each one. Glad and Walter, their wedding day; Maggie, age four; Gladiola and Maggie, Maggie's high school graduation; Walter-Glad-Maggie Abernathy, Cape Cod. When I'd finished going through the photos, Dad took them.

The breeze kicked up, and the late-afternoon sun casted orange and red shadows in the distance. No one asked about leaving. No one suggested or considered it.

Our folding chairs—the pews.

The cemetery—the sanctuary.

The stories shared—the scripture.

The silent moments between us—a time of reflection.

The urn—a time capsule of memories to be buried in a special place for safekeeping.

Maggie finally stood, bowed her head, and recited the Lord's Prayer. When her gaze met Bradley's, he placed Glad's urn in the ground.

Maggie and Bradley held hands and stared into the ground. Maggie reached for me, and I rested my head on her shoulder while Dad folded up the chairs and returned them to the trunk of the car.

"Families, relationships, and people aren't perfect. Nothing is." Maggie squeezed my fingers. "When people leave, perspectives change—yet again." She gazed at Bradley, then at me. "Don't be afraid of imperfection. Embrace it. The love you invest will return. Maybe not in the way you think it should or from an obvious person or in a timely fashion, but it'll come back when you need it most."

Dad placed his hands on my shoulders, his whispers comforting. I imagined Glad standing next to me, holding my hand.

"Mom. Nana wouldn't want us to spend *too* much time staring into this dark hole."

"You're right." Maggie took a gladiola that was as white as snow from the vase and placed it in the grave. "I love you, Mom. I'll be seeing you."

I chose a yellow one, Dad chose a red, and Red

chose a pastel stalk with blooms the color of orange sherbet. We filled the hole with blossoms as vibrant as the woman we loved.

"You're in my heart forever. You'll always be *my* Gladiola. Lil and Grace will know you through me. I'm keeping your reading glasses for the future. I might need them."

"I know you'll be watching over me," Dad said. "You can ride on the back of my horse anytime."

"You were caring, funny, and tough when you needed to be. The sparkle in your eyes made me believe I could achieve anything with hard work and compassion. You were and always will be the best Nana." Bradley took the remaining gladiolas from the vases, handed them to his mom, and kissed her cheek. "And when I think Nana's *really* gone, I'll look to you—and she'll be there."

CHAPTER 23

AFTER HAVING DINNER on the patio at the Goldsterns, I helped Judy and Maggie clear the dishes. Matt had called before he gave Lil and Gracie their bath. They blew me kisses through the phone screen, and I wished them sweet dreams.

Maggie found me on the front porch.

"Can I join you?"

Matt had finalized his plans with Branch and was leaving the day after we returned home. Matt made it clear that prolonging his departure wouldn't be good for any of us. I thought about Glad's ashes in the hole, the vases of gladiolas, the photos, and the stories of her life, the service, and the bagpiper's tunes that gave me goose bumps and made me start a bucket list of travels, starting with Scotland.

"Apparently, everyone is the catalyst of their own story." I picked at my thumbnail.

"Yep. Pretty much." Maggie sipped her wine and kicked off her sandals.

"So, while I've spent my time pretending to be

the puppet master, as Matt says, of the cast of characters in my life, I've failed to see the only strings I control are my own."

"Wow, that must've been some phone call."

"Matt's leaving for Wyoming the day after we get back."

"This probably isn't what you want to hear, but working for Branch might be what's best," she said. "Matt'll be able to grow his herd. Isn't that what you wanted?"

"Yes. I'd like to blame Tristan, but I know his friendship with Branch has nothing to do with Matt's decision."

Two young boys on scooters raced down the center of the empty street, whooping and hollering about who would win the race home.

"I'm sure Matt has weighed his decision carefully, and you're right, you can't blame Tristan. The only strings you control are your own." Maggie raised her glass and sipped her wine. "It's funny how we think we can control things we can't or even want to. We don't get to choose the actions or reactions of others. We can choose only for ourselves. And when we do, we need to understand that we're all connected and our choices, whatever they may be, will affect somebody somewhere somehow. And when it's all said and done, you have to do what's right—*for you*."

"Maggie."

"Yeah, Chloe."

"How many glasses of wine have you had?"

"Not enough." She narrowed her gaze at the white electric sports car parking in front of the house. "I thought I'd be okay with this. It's been such a long time." She raised her glass to the two men getting out of the car.

"Is that?" I glanced at her with wide eyes.

"Yes. I told Bradley I'd be fine with seeing Beckett. I'm not so sure. I haven't seen Bradley's dad in…" She drummed her fingers on the arm of the rattan loveseat. "I don't know when. And the kick is, my ex-husband has ended up with the designer who redecorated my house after we got divorced. Paul Mitchell."

Beckett's hair had grayed, and he sported a goatee. He was dressed in pressed jeans and a crisp white linen shirt. His partner, Paul, wore salmon trousers, a stark white tee, and moccasin-type shoes exuding dollar signs.

Maggie greeted them. Beckett's reserved attitude made me wonder if he'd been quiet when he was married to Maggie.

"This is Chloe. Chloe, this is Beckett. And this is Paul."

"Hi, Beckett. I remember you. The last time I saw you, I was just a kid. Maybe seven or eight."

"You've certainly grown up. Bradley tells me you have twin girls."

"I do. Lil and Gracie. They're back home with…" I tucked my fingers into the front pockets of my jeans, thinking how to end my sentence without leaving myself open for questions. "With their dad. Nice to meet you, Paul."

Maggie invited Beckett and Paul to join us on the patio in the backyard.

"I'll show you the shortcut," I said. "Bradley and Red are with my dad and our friend, Pink." I led Beckett and Paul through an archway covered with purple blooms at the side of the house. Paul commented on the Goldsterns' beautiful Tudor home and luscious hydrangea bushes, ivy, and flowers fit for a prize garden show.

Dad greeted Beckett with a handshake. "Maggie said you'd be stopping by. It's nice to see you again."

Bradley met his father with a pat on the back. Red greeted Beckett and Paul with hugs. She was a hugger. She could get right in there. Me, I hesitated, opening my arms to the unknown proved to be a hurdle when it came to getting close to people. I needed time, and the time I needed seemed to be a pitfall when it came to being vulnerable.

"Hope we're not intruding," Beckett said, eyeing the crowd.

"Not at all. We're getting ready for dessert and after-dinner drinks. Perfect timing," Pink said.

Beckett told my father he couldn't believe I was all grown up and so beautiful.

My gaze met Bradley's, and I raised my brow. "If you'll excuse me, I'll go help Judy and Maggie." My cheeks warmed: the uncomfortable feeling trickled through my veins.

Maggie and Judy stood at the sink, peering through the kitchen window. "What's going on in here?" I whispered even though no one was around.

"Beckett wanted to stop by to give his condolences. I can't believe he's with Paul. They're pretty serious." Maggie paused. "I remember accusing Beckett of having an affair with Paul the summer after the divorce. I was so angry. They'd met at a retirement party for one of Beckett's colleagues in the art department. And look at them now. Who would've thought a twenty-something-year marriage would lead us in totally opposite happily ever after directions?"

Maggie and Judy scurried away from the window.

"They saw us gawking at them, didn't they?" Maggie ducked.

"Clearly," Judy replied. "We're not as sneaky as we used to be."

"Beckett being here shouldn't be a big deal." Maggie shook out her hands and danced in a circle.

"Yep. No big deal. The only strings you can control are your own. Way to shake it off, Mags." I took a cold beer from the fridge and popped the top.

"Touché." Maggie sipped her wine. "Chloe, you carry my wine, and I'll get the cake. I wouldn't want Beckett to think—"

"Who cares what Beckett thinks?" Judy picked up the tray of dessert plates. "You have a cowboy out there with your name on him."

I winced. "Child present. I don't need to hear everything you're thinking, and this is why people shouldn't get married."

"What?" Judy said.

"Discussion for another day," I said. "I don't think there's enough beer."

"Ah, but remember *the holes*." Maggie raised her glass.

"What?" Judy said louder.

"When we lose someone, it leaves a hole. And

as we age, if we're lucky enough, we find someone who fills the holes of those we've lost. Like Maggie filled my mom's void when I was younger, and Glad filled the holes Dad's mom left when she died."

"That's sweet," Judy said. "Let's go before our entrance is beyond awkward. By the way, you two need to curb the alcohol."

"Too late." I nudged them out the door to the patio.

The evening turned into a long one. Once Maggie found her footing, conversation flowed and so did the cocktails. Beckett spoke about teaching art history at Wayne State and his acquired passion for Thai cooking.

"On Mondays, two other couples join us for cooking class at a little place on the other side of town." He straightened his shoulders and sipped his martini, shaken not stirred.

"It's fabulous." Paul kissed his pinched fingers, then flicked them into the air like a gourmet chef who'd served his finest meal. "Last week, we made Tom Kha. To die—"

"For," Beckett said. "Sour, spicy, head-on shrimp, coconut milk. To die—"

"For," Paul said.

Beckett and Paul finished each other's thoughts

the entire conversation. Beckett leaned toward Maggie. "If it weren't for you, I wouldn't have connected with Paul."

I leaned in from the other side. "Holes."

She raised her glass to toast. "Here's to holes."

"To holes," everyone said in unison.

Beckett and Paul shrugged as they pretended to know what we were talking about. They clinked their glasses together and said, "Here's to filling the holes."

Judy lit citronella candles after the sun set. We lounged in the glow, discussing travel plans, children, and Glad. Beckett excused himself, then returned with a gift.

"Before we go, this is for you." Beckett handed Maggie a package wrapped in pink silk tied with a flouncy satin ribbon.

Maggie untied the ribbon, and the silk fabric slid away from an antique picture frame. Her downturned lips lifted, and her eyes glistened.

"I cleaned out some boxes in the attic and found it. Perfect timing. I thought you should have it." Beckett raised his glass. "To Glad."

"To Glad," we all said in unison.

Maggie showed everyone the framed photo of her, Glad, and a young Bradley sitting on the beach. The trio of redheads laughed into the camera on a perfect sunny day.

"Thank you, Beckett." Maggie stood, opened her arms, and Beckett slid in for a hug. She then kissed his cheek. Red wiped the corners of her eyes. What had ended with hurt feelings, question, and a broken marriage for the two was in the past. According to my mom's best friend and business partner, Hermione Crow, broken circles could be repaired. Circles were meant to intersect and bring individuals together.

Their circle was certainly complete.

"You're welcome, Maggie." He held her hands in his. "When do you return to the ranch?"

"Tomorrow evening. Guess it's time to get used to another normal. Thanks for stopping by." Her gaze met his partner's. "Thank you, Paul."

"One last toast before we leave." Beckett raised an almost empty cocktail. "Here's to one woman's story who influenced so many women's journeys."

"To Glad," we all said again, except Maggie.

"To my favorite Gladiola. Somehow, the stars seem brighter tonight." She glanced toward heaven, drained her wineglass, and sat next to my dad.

"They most certainly do." Dad held her close.

Dad had Maggie. Bradley had Red. Beckett had Paul. Judy had Pink.

I would soon have no one.

CHAPTER 24

D AD GRIPPED THE steering wheel with one hand and held Maggie's hand with the other on the deserted two-lane road back to the ranch. Besides an occasional glance between them, their unspoken conversation was one of love and understanding. I stared out the back seat window, thinking about the changes I faced and missing Bradley's company. He and Red had stayed on with his dad in Michigan for an additional two days before flying back to Boston.

My heart raced as we neared the ranch. I couldn't wait to hug the girls. The three days away felt like weeks. Facing Matt negated the feelings I'd started to have about getting married, and he'd never know now that he'd signed on with Branch. If working for Branch presented an opportunity he couldn't pass up, I wouldn't be the one to ruin it, since I'd been the one to screw up our relationship.

Dad parked the Suburban in front of the main house. The empty porch only reminded me of Glad's absence. Even the dinner bell looked lonely.

Who would take over Glad's duty of calling us to the table? The sting behind my eyes was as painful as the day she passed away. My disbelief had been replaced with a numbing ache. Dad's gaze met mine in the rearview mirror.

Maggie shuffled up the front stairs and went inside. Dad and I unloaded the bags.

"Is Maggie going to be okay?" I left my bag at the stairs of the porch.

"Not for a while. Grief is strange. The waves will hit hard." Dad kissed my forehead.

By the time we got inside, Maggie had unpacked her backpack and put the photo Beckett had given her on the hand-hewn mantel of the stone fireplace in the living room.

"Oh, Mom. Things just aren't going to be the same without you." Maggie kissed her fingers and touched the frame.

"I'll leave you two alone." I kissed Dad's bristly cheek and made my way home. I shuffled up the back stairs with my bag that seemed doubly heavy and opened the mudroom door. The house was strangely still.

"Hello." No one answered. I peeked into the empty living room. I ran my hand over the mantel decorated with silver horseshoes and fiddled with my bandanna. The ache I harbored for Glad didn't mask the hole Matt's absence had created, and he hadn't even left yet.

Matt's leather duffels were in the corner of the room. I unzipped one of the bags, took out his denim jacket, and replaced it with a small black-and-white framed photo of the girls that I'd wrapped in my denim jacket. He'd need something to fill the hole, too.

The sound of wagon wheels against the gravel drive took my attention from something I couldn't change and had accepted to something I gladly welcomed. I zipped up Matt's duffel, stashed his jacket in the laundry room, and hurried outside.

"Well, isn't this a sight," I hollered.

"Whoa," Sarah bellowed, pulling back on Butch and Sundance's reins.

Emma's smiling face popped up over her mom's shoulder. Gracie and Lil climbed out of Maria's arms and reached for me.

"Y'all look like you're having fun." I ran my fingers through Butch's sandy-colored mane. "Sure is a fancy ride."

"Tristan taught Mom how to drive the wagon," Emma said.

"I already knew. He just thinks he taught me how." Sarah tipped her cowboy hat and winked.

"Hope you weren't worried," Maria said. "I

thought we'd be back before you got home, but someone went wading in the creek." She pointed to Gracie. "She's wet."

"Fun." Gracie clapped.

"She couldn't wait for me to take off my boots and roll up my pants." Maria hopped out of the wagon and shook out her legs.

"Looks like you went in, too." With open arms, I took my soaked girl. "Holy cow. You're dripping." I wasn't sure how keen I was on the girls playing in the river without Matt or me around.

Emma jumped from the wagon bed to help Maria and Lil down the steps.

"I see the look in your eye," Sarah said. "Us mommas can be pretty protective. When Matt gave us the go-ahead, we promised we wouldn't go beyond the shallow bend just past the willow."

"I guess I'm gonna have to get used to my girls exploring the world when I'm not around." Someday, they'd be with their father and I'd have to trust they'd be okay.

"Sarah and I both have radios if that'll help ease your mind." Maria counted heads, then tickled Lil's belly until she laughed.

"I'll be back after I take care of the horses. Emma, are you staying or going?" Sarah handed me the radio clipped to her belt.

"Going." Emma climbed onto the wagon's bench.

Sarah resumed her position in the driver's seat, took the reins, and released the brake. "Gypsy will be glad you're back." With a click of her tongue, they left.

"Come on, G. Let's get cleaned up. No more going in the river." I held the mudroom door open for Maria and Lil. Gracie played with my hair and blew bubbles with the saliva she'd collected in the seam of her lips. Her sloppy kiss on my cheek made not having Glad here a little better.

Holes.

After peeling wet clothing off my daughter, I bathed her and dressed her in a clean tee and denim bibs embroidered with sunflowers. Maria and Lil's voices trailed upstairs. Maria's patient tone sounded like she'd been parenting for years. Her kindness and structure would be great assets in the classroom once she finished her college courses.

Gracie and I went downstairs to the living room.

"Momma," Lil called.

I set Gracie on the Navajo rug Matt had given me for my birthday. The reds and gold-flaxen hues wouldn't be so vibrant without him. I plopped down on the sofa. Lil crawled into my lap.

"So, what have I missed?" I touched my nose to Lil's.

"The usual. Crying, laughing, eating, messes that needed cleaning up, new teeth," Maria said.

"New teeth?" I checked Gracie's mouth. "So close to a full set of chompers." I showed the girls my teeth, and they showed me theirs.

"Naps were pretty regular. I'm sure they're tired."

"I'm tired, too."

"How'd everything go?" Maria asked.

Gracie ran a plastic horse down my leg. "Go, go, go."

"It went. Sad. Busy. Saw old friends. Bradley was great. Went out to dinner at a fancy restaurant. The kind with real silverware and crystal wineglasses. There weren't any high chairs or babies. I sure did miss you guys." I ruffled Gracie's hair.

"We missed you, too." Maria smiled.

"What do you say I put you two little ladies in Pop-Pop's wagon and we go see Gypsy?" I paused. "Thank you so much for taking care of the girls. I don't know what I'd do without you." I rummaged through my leather satchel for the Celtic vase I'd gotten her at an iconic pottery house in Detroit as a thank-you. I handed her a white box tied with a teal ribbon. "A little something from the D."

Maria opened the gift. "It's beautiful. I love the iridescent turquoise sheen." She read the card.

"Something to keep your wildflowers in," I said.

"We had a fun time. Sarah and Emma really helped out, and Matt was great. He said Lil woke up the night before last, screaming. When I got here in the morning, he was asleep in the chair with her."

"Probably the teeth." I pushed myself up and helped the girls toddle outside. They sat on the stoop and waited for me to get their wagon. When I returned, a cow was in the yard.

"Where'd you come from?" I scanned the area for additional strays. "We haven't had stray calves in a long time. Guess I should tell the guys to check the fencing."

Maria came out and shut the door. "Whoa. Where'd the cow come from?"

"Cow." Lil pointed and mooed.

"Maybe she'll follow us." I helped Gracie and Lil into the wagon.

"Chances are good." Maria ran inside and returned with the satchel of animal treats and a rope we kept in the mudroom. "You want me to stay for a bit?"

"Nope. You need a break. See you the day after tomorrow."

Maria got into her Jeep, rolled down the window, and waved goodbye.

After petting the stray, I held her face in my hands. "All you have to do is follow me, and we'll get you home." I fed her a palmful of cattle cubes, put the rope around her neck, then gave her more treats.

"Momma," Gracie called.

"I haven't forgotten you, baby girl." I held the lead in one hand and the wagon handle in the other. It took me a bit to coax the stray along the gravel drive. Gypsy grazed in the pasture adjacent to the barn. Her chin rested on the fence rail. Gracie and Lil mooed.

"I've got myself a herd," I called to Sarah, who came to help me.

"You sure do." She kicked caked mud from the soles of her boots.

The stray straggled behind, keeping her distance.

Tristan came from the barn. "What're you doing here?"

"I live here." I stopped at the pen closest to the houses.

"I meant the cow." He slapped his gloves against his chaps. "Never ends, but you already know that." He took the cow's lead from me. "Come on. We'll put you in the pen on the other side of the corral since Gypsy's in this one."

Emma skipped out of the barn. "All done, Mom."

"Has Gypsy been a good girl?" I inspected the wrap on her leg, then stroked her black mane. She nibbled sugar from my hand, and I told her she was beautiful.

"Yes." Sarah patted Gypsy's neck. "It's time to let her enjoy the pasture, and we'll go from there."

"As long as she's here, it's all good. We'll have to learn how to navigate our relationship without the cattle, wild rides, and midnight meetings," I said.

"Patience is key." Sarah took Emma's hand.

Tristan's gaze met Sarah's. Emma had her eye on something more than the girls and the horses.

"I appreciate everything you've done. Maria told me how helpful you were while I was gone. Thank you." Hugging might not have been my usual nature, but I figured I better start since I'd be needing some now that my Gladiola had gone and Matt wouldn't be warming the bed, swatting me with his superhero cape made from a bath towel or telling corny cowboy jokes while doing dinner dishes. There was something in Sarah's comforting hug that softened the wall I'd built to protect myself.

Emma entertained the girls with a game of peek-a-boo.

"I told you I raised her alone. I left out the details though." Sarah watched her daughter. "When she was four, her father left us. It's been eight years. His dreams revolved around the rodeo. Not me or Em. When he left, she shut down. Skipping out of the barn and seeing her open up does my heart good. She's been talking so much more. She loves visiting the ranch." Sarah beamed. "Look at her. Being here has done more for her than the pediatrician, speech therapist, and two psychologists we've seen. I worry about her teenage years we're heading into." She paused. "You probably didn't need the whole story."

"I'm glad you told me. Now I understand why she loves the horses, especially my Huckleberry. Can I ask you something though?"

"Sure," she said.

"Do you ever wish Emma's father were around?"

"Truth?"

"Yes." I fiddled with a splinter of jagged wood

on the fence rail.

"I wanted to be a family so badly. I thought if he stayed, he would've learned to love us. I don't think so now." She glanced down. "I know so. Sure, I'd like him to be around, but I also know it wouldn't be good for us. His lifestyle wouldn't exactly be a positive influence."

Holes, I thought to myself. "I'm sorry," I said.

"You can call me any time, Chloe, and I don't mean just for help with the animals."

"Thanks, I appreciate that."

Emma pulled the wagon in circles, entertaining the girls. I wasn't the only one who'd built walls. We all had walls to some degree. Emma locked gazes with Gypsy, then went to her. There was a silent understanding between them, something gentle and accepting. I'd seen it early on and knew I had to bring horses and people together. Gypsy rested her head on Emma's shoulder when she reached in for a snuggle.

I wasn't the only one who needed animals. Emma's message was loud and clear. Purpose wasn't decided by outside forces. Purpose came from within. Purpose was unspoken and vulnerable to change.

CHAPTER 25

THE LONG DAY of traveling home, playing with the girls, and the prospect of saying goodbye to Matt weighed me down. After tucking the girls in, I joined him in the living room. With our feet on the ottoman, the crackling fire filled the stillness between us. Our silent conversation possessed a different intonation than Dad and Maggie's had during the drive back to the ranch.

"Will you call? The girls would like that."

"Yes." He rested his head against the sofa cushion. "I'll be back to visit, and you can bring the girls down. We'll make a schedule once I get settled."

"They'll like that." I focused on the dying fire.

"Can you please look at me?" he asked.

Another hole bore its way into the part of me I tried so hard to control and protect. I stared at my fuzzy socks. There were no studs to count, no tissue to crumple.

"Let's not spend tonight in silence. That's not us." He put his arm around my shoulder.

"I don't think there's much to talk about. We both know what's happening here."

"I won't give you a yellow rose. I won't tell you I love you."

"Probably best." I held his gaze. "I know you have to go."

IN THE MORNING, Matt packed his truck and loaded Trigger into the horse trailer. Lola hopped into the passenger's seat and stared at us from the cab window. Matt said goodbye to the girls, then me. As much as I knew I should air my feelings, I couldn't. Branch hadn't offered him a lifetime commitment, but the money and cattle would further Matt's dream of growing a significant herd. I wouldn't take another dream away from him. He kissed my cheek and got into the truck.

Why were feelings so damned hard?

Dad's disappointed expression sent a silent message I couldn't respond to. With Lil holding one hand and Gracie holding the other, we watched Matt drive away. The girls and I were ready to begin a different life. Tires against the gravel drive left dusty clouds that would soon settle like distant memories.

"Let's go see the horses. They make everything

better." I squeezed the girls' fingers.

"Gypsy," Gracie shouted.

"You said my girl's name." I crouched. "Yay. You said her name."

Lil hugged her sister.

The girls took their usual spots in Pop-Pop's wagon. I handed each of them a dandelion from the yard, and we headed to the barn. They tickled each other with the soft petals.

I opened the gate to the pasture and pulled the wagon close to the pond. The bumps and dips prodded boisterous belly laughs that lifted the bits of sadness I carried. Gracie climbed from the wagon and inspected each step she took. There was something to be said for minding her way, and I took note. Lil's longing gaze and open arms hinted she wasn't ready to be as independent as her sister, so I helped her like I wanted to help Emma and others.

Casanova's whinny announced Tristan's arrival. He rode in with his brother, Justin, dismounted, and disappeared into the barn.

Lil handed me a rock. "Thank you. It's very pretty." I held it in the palm of my hand. "Rock. Can you say rock?" She handed me another one.

Gracie toddled over, took the stone, and inspected it. "Rock."

Lil took it from her and dropped it in the water, then Gracie kissed her cheek.

Gracie's eyes got big, and she pointed to Tristan who marched toward us. Gracie's frown matched his.

"Hey," he called.

"Hey."

"We need a man on a horse."

"Where are Silas and Quinn?"

"They're in town. Your dad's busy. He's designated you. Since it's Maria's day off, Maggie's waiting for you to bring the girls to the main house." Tristan slapped his gloves against his thigh. He pointed to Lil.

"No," Gracie said to Lil. "No eat."

I lifted Lil to my hip.

"Anything hurt when you did that?" Tristan lowered his gaze.

I shook my head and helped the girls back into the wagon.

"Just checking. Justin's saddling up Big Red for you. I'll meet you in the barn." He handed me a radio. "We need you, bosslady."

"I need you, too." I held Tristan's gaze. With Bradley and Red back in Boston and the barn reno winding down, I'd be back in the saddle wrangling the cattle like I should've been all along regardless of what I wanted. "Why Big Red?"

"Because it's his turn. We're down to half the herd now that you've been on a mission to find them acceptable homes. He's looking forward to the ride."

"Five more are going next week. Found a family near Livingston with a brood of young wranglers looking for smooth rides." I patted my pocket. Gypsy eyed me from the pen. "Twenty seems like nothing now. Go see your horse, then let's get a move on."

"Gypsy." Gracie blew her a kiss.

"Hello, girl." Gypsy pushed her nose into my belly, begging for the sugar in my hand. I patted her chest. "I've got work to do. It won't be the same without you."

"Gypsy." Gracie stood up in the wagon.

Lil blew her a kiss, then tugged at her sister's hand until she sat.

Gypsy pressed her chest against the fence. She knew as much as I did that she couldn't come with me. I said my goodbyes and told her I'd be back later. I gripped the wagon handle and headed for the main house.

At the house, Maggie waited in the yard.

"What's Dad doing today?"

"Business," she said. "You get yourself ready. I

got the girls." Maggie hoisted Lil to her hip and held Gracie's hand.

"What kind of business?"

"The kind of business that gets you on a horse and back in the pasture. We're short-handed—now go."

The girls and Maggie managed the steps without me and went inside.

I hustled home, grabbed my gear, hopped into Grandpa's old pickup, and got myself to the barn. The hum of the engine settled the nervous knots in my gut. This kind of quiet made for an open mind and sharp senses. I stopped at the gate and glanced over to the empty passenger's seat.

What are you waiting for?

The undeniable voice sent a shiver up my spine. Glad wasn't here, but she was.

"I don't know." I eased off the brake, and the truck lurched forward. A pair of pink speckled readers from beneath the passenger's seat slid across the floor. I leaned over, grabbed the glasses, then tucked them into my shirt pocket.

Before saddling up, I went into the office, scanned the list of horses, and highlighted five more. Finding them homes would take us down to fifteen, which didn't seem possible. I tacked the list to the corkboard. As hard as it was to say goodbye to the horses I loved, I couldn't keep them. They had forever homes, and I needed to let them live their best lives.

'Twas the season of letting go.

I leafed through the mail on the desk. A return address caught my eye, and I ripped open the envelope. The Richardson Foundation had rejected my grant proposal. I crumpled up the form letter and tossed it in the garbage.

Rounding up strays with Tristan and Justin became more than labor intensive. Big Red's lack of regular riding proved to be hard work as well. He needed prodding and praise like the rest of us. After a long day, I enjoyed the rhythm of his canter as we raced home.

I had Big Red's saddle off and put away before Tristan and Justin rode in.

"You're certainly in a hurry." Justin tied Belle to the hitching post.

"Would you mind cleaning him up? I'd really like to get the girls home and ready for bed at a decent hour." I fed Big Red a carrot and praised his efforts.

"Seems to me you've got more on your mind than getting Gracie and Lil ready for bed." Justin took the bridle. "Go on."

I hopped in the truck, took off my cowboy hat,

and drove to the main house, which wasn't far, but driving Grandpa's truck was magical and settled stormy feelings. I took Glad's readers from my pocket and put them on my head as if they were mine.

"That was more than riding out there today, Gladiola. It was therapy. I know what I have to do." I pulled up to the main house, beeped the horn, and turned off the engine.

Maggie came outside with the girls.

"You're welcome to stay for dinner." She sat in one of the rocking chairs.

"I appreciate the offer, but I should take the girls home. We all need a bath, something to eat, and jammies. Come on, girls." I pointed to the truck. "I left the keys in the ignition."

"What's with the glasses?" Maggie helped the girls maneuver down the front steps.

"They were under the seat in the truck. Thought wearing them would make me feel better."

"These were in the baking cupboard next to the oven." Maggie took the gold-rimmed glasses from the collar of her tee.

"I have a feeling we'll be finding glasses a lot."

"Only our Gladiola," Maggie said with a smile.

I got my hat from Grandpa's truck and put it

on Gracie. She held the brim and waved. Maggie blew her kisses. Back at the house, I kicked my boots off at the mudroom door, got the girls inside and settled in their high chairs. Gracie pounded on the empty tray.

"I'm going as fast as I can." I cut up a banana. Lil ate the sweet slices, and her sister stacked them into a tower and knocked them over. I cut up bite-sized pieces of roasted chicken and cheese.

I dialed the phone. The girls ate, and I hoped they'd go to sleep easily when the time came. When my mom didn't answer, I left a message and hung up.

Gracie devoured the last few nibbles of food. I washed her sticky face and hands, then got her out of the high chair. She pulled at Lil's feet, hurrying her along.

"Why don't you help me finish my dinner?" I patted my leg, and Gracie accepted the invite. When I opened my mouth, she fed me like a momma bird until my plate was empty. I handed Gracie my napkin, and she wiped my lips.

Lil finished her dinner, too, smacked her lips, and showed me empty hands.

"Let's go, ladies. A bath and ready for bed."

I checked the message machine. There was nothing from Matt.

"Daddy will call." I wondered if Sarah had said the same thing to Emma after her father had left.

Upstairs, my bedroom at the end of the hall appeared darker than usual. I'd never dreamed that Matt would veer at the fork in the road, but he had. I bathed the girls, rocked them, read them the story about the lost pony, then tucked them in. Quiet babble turned to sleepy breaths of slumber. Sitting on my bed, I dialed the phone. My hands shook as I waited for Sarah to answer.

"Hi, Sarah. It's Chloe McIntyre. Hope I'm not bothering you."

"Not at all."

"I was wondering if you knew anyone who knows about animal therapy and writing grants." I ran my fingers through my hair.

"As in animals working with people?"

"Yes. Animals working with people, children with emotional setbacks and deficits. Emma has inspired me to expand the ranch's purpose. I received a rejection today and need human help."

Sarah didn't say anything.

"Are you there?"

"I'm sorry," she replied.

"I didn't mean to upset you."

"Quite the opposite. I've been watching her, too. I've made every excuse to spend time at your place, but you already know that."

"I don't know anyone. I can talk to Doc Kneely."

"I'd appreciate it." I said good night and ended the call.

I'd built a wall, had numerous excuses why marriage wasn't for me, suggested a prenup of all things, and proposed to Matt for the wrong reasons. I'd focused on everything around me when what I really needed was to focus on myself—just like Matt had said—and I'd refused.

I imagined the 617 Ranch with a corral of gentle horses, animals with angels' wings, surrounded by children of all ages who needed support, and I was the nucleus, craving interaction with similar souls. I wanted to create a program that bred self-esteem and communication through the love of animals. I wanted to change my ways as much as I wanted to help others.

After showering and putting on my pajamas, I settled beneath the cool sheets and downy comforter. I prayed. Moonlight danced across the ceiling, and hope crept into my darkest places.

Gracie's shriek pierced the quiet. I kicked off the covers and rushed to get her before she could wake Lil.

"Momma's here." I brought her to my room to

cuddle. My heavy eyelids drifted shut, and she patted my cheek. "Go to sleep, Gracie." I held her hand. When her babble stopped, Lil's cry stirred us both.

CHAPTER 26

THE GIRLS AND I hunkered down in my bed around 2:00 a.m. We tossed and turned. Their tube of numbing gel for tender gums was empty, and I contemplated inventing numbing gel for a hurting heart, but someone had already taken that idea and called it bourbon.

I woke to Lil's touch. Gracie sat on the floor with the latest magazine featuring my mother and her current clothing collection. I got up, sat with her, and smoothed out the wrinkled torn pages.

"Coco." Gracie pointed to the photograph of my mother.

"Yes. That's our Coco."

I slipped into my jeans and a clean shirt, then toted the girls into the bathroom to wash up, brush my hair, and gargle. The medicinal mouth wash jarred my sleepy senses. The girls emptied the tub toys tote and played. Ignoring the mess, I ushered them into the hallway and we headed downstairs. Maria rushed in through the mudroom door.

"Sorry I'm late. Did you get my message? A

neighbor helped me fix the flat tire." She fanned her cheeks.

I listened to the archaic answering machine that had belonged to my grandpa. I'd insisted on keeping it even though Matt made fun of the antique. It wasn't high-tech, but I liked pushing the button and listening to the messages. "Now I have." I blew hair away from my face. "We just got up. We had a rough night. These two need breakfast. Actually, they need everything." I checked the messages again. Matt hadn't called.

"On it." Maria buckled the girls into their high chairs.

I ate toast over the sink. Crumbs fell into my grandmother's farmhouse basin that I'd restored. I struggled with letting go of *things*, too. Sentiment evoked from things felt safer than emotion. They made me feel close to those I loved. The saddle my granddad had given me for my sixteenth birthday never let me down. The necklace I'd lost in the river stayed with me and never doubted my wildest wishes. The miniature horseshoe Matt had given me—lost too.

My thoughts took a sharp left turn. If I lost everything, how would I know I was loved? I crammed the last bit of toast in my mouth. Getting outside was imperative.

"I have to go. Featherstone is here." I yawned, kissed the girls, slipped on my boots, and left.

He parked his truck and got out. He wore his usual black wide-brimmed hat and a thick braid down the middle of his back. We reviewed the day's agenda, then met Gypsy at the fence.

She ate the treat from my hand and buried her nose in my belly. Dad made his way out of the barn.

"Morning," I said.

"Morning. There's a message from Sarah on the desk and one from a fellow inquiring about horses. You're doing a fine job whittling down the herd. I know how hard it is for you to let go. Getting you back in the pasture full-time is a win for all of us." He patted my shoulder, then greeted Mr. Featherstone with a handshake.

"I told you I wouldn't let you down." But I already had, now that Matt was gone.

"I'll leave you two to your work." He mounted Breeze and rode away.

I shuffled into the office, plunked myself in the chair, and read the phone messages Dad had taken. Sarah had found two young cattle dogs in need of a home. I dialed her number on the landline. "Hey, Sarah, cattle dogs?"

"Yep. Thought you might be interested. I know

you're cutting back on horses, but the cattle aren't going anywhere. And with Matt in Wyoming with Lola, I thought you could use the dogs. Who doesn't love reliable, cheap help? The rancher sold his place and can't take them. His name is Beau Reeves."

"If you give me his number, I'll check them out. I'd like to meet them before making any promises. I'll keep you posted. Any leads on a grant writer?"

"No. But if I run across someone, I'll let you know."

With the dwindling number of horses and the loss of Matt, cutting back hardly described a transition I'd never fathomed.

Dad hadn't mentioned filling Matt's position, and not hiring a new wrangler would mean more budget to work with when it came to a therapy center. Would it be possible I wouldn't need a grant to get this project off the ground? Money or no money, no one could fill Matt's boots.

I took the two-way radio from the cradle and walked over to the old barn. The lower level was completed, including the bathroom. The reconfigured roomier stalls were an easy in and easy out through the wider aisle, the tack room ready to be organized and filled.

Upstairs, the work crew discussed the rafters.

The ceiling had been cleaned and sealed. The blue sky shone through the skylights. I snapped a few pictures on my phone, loaded them into a text to Matt, then deleted the message. He didn't need a reminder of the priorities that drove us apart.

"Like what you see?" Mr. Cortright adjusted his tool belt.

"Sure do. What's next?"

"Light fixtures and the bar." He picked up a ladder and walked to the opposite end of the barn.

My phone rang, and Matt's picture appeared on the screen. The call cut out as soon as I answered.

"Remind me to ask Featherstone for a landline out here," I said to myself, hustling downstairs and over to the other barn to call him back from the office. Before I dialed, the phone rang. Surely, Matt would be on the other end.

"Chloe, is that you?"

I pinched the bridge of my nose. "Hi, Mom. Why are you calling the barn?"

"That's some greeting. It's nice to hear your voice, too. Maria told me I might catch you there, and I'm returning your call."

"Sorry, I thought you were someone else. How are you?"

"I'm fine. Who were you expecting?"

"I don't want to say," I replied.

"If you're busy, I can call later."

"That might be better. I've got an errand to run and some stuff to do for Dad." As much as I wanted to tell her about Matt, I couldn't. "Can we talk later? I'll need more than a few minutes."

"You sound strange."

"There's a lot going on." I leaned against the office wall.

"I heard about Glad. I'm sorry. I know how close you two were."

"How?" I hadn't told her about Glad yet. Who had she been talking to?

"We'll talk this evening. I promise I'll answer."

"Bye, Mom." I hung up the receiver.

Matt had surely called to talk to Gracie and Lil. I'd call him later when the girls and I were together. I read Sarah's note again, then called Beau Reeves, the rancher wanting to find a home for his cattle dogs. They were on the young side, trained, and healthy. I jotted down the directions to his place in case cell service wasn't available and told him I'd make the thirty-minute drive after I checked in with Maria.

Before setting the phone receiver in the cradle, I contemplated calling Matt again, then hung up.

"This is one of those times a girl needs her

momma," I said to myself.

"I kind of figured that, so here I am. Surprise."

I turned around to see my mother standing in the doorway. "What are you doing here? How? When?" I squeezed her tight and she squealed. How lucky I was to have her back in my life!

"I could say I'm here on business, but your dad told me about Glad."

"What else did Dad tell you?"

"That you're going through a rough patch. You can fill me in later." She sat on the corner of the desk—her designer cowboy boots appeared to be freshly buffed. "Tell me about the canines you're rescuing." She wound her long blonde hair into a knotted bun. "I couldn't help but overhear your conversation."

"I haven't taken them in yet. I'd like to see if they're as promising as they sound."

"I have no doubt you'll whip them into shape in no time. It's not like you to turn down an animal in need."

"I can't believe you're here."

"I was worried. I wanted to be here for you because that's what mothers do. I've turned over a new leaf. Remember? I also know you lost a wrangler. Probably the most important one." She tucked her hands in the back of her unusually plain jeans. "I suspect you thought I was Matt on the phone. Sorry to disappoint you."

"It's been tough. I miss Glad." I bit my lip and lowered my gaze. "And I missed Matt before he even left."

"I'm not used to seeing you like this." The corner of her lip turned down. She opened her arms, and I melted into her. "You're breaking my heart."

"Mom." I rested my chin on her shoulder and let her iconic perfume take me to a happier place.

"You'll figure this out. I have no doubt."

"The girls need their daddy." I sniffled and held her gaze.

"Kind of like someone else I know. You've always needed your daddy." She straightened my bandanna. "I love this scarf on you."

"Thanks. It's one of yours."

"Correction. It's one of *our* designs. And you make it beautiful." She caressed my cheeks. "What do you say we go rescue some dogs?"

"Mom, did Dad ask you to visit?" I grabbed the truck keys from the desk and tucked my phone into my back pocket.

"No. He didn't. There was something in your voice in that last message, and I figured it was time to make a trip to see you."

CHAPTER 27

THE DRIVE TO Mr. Reeves's ranch went quickly as I allowed my woes to flow. I told my mom about the trip to Michigan to bury Glad's ashes, Bradley and Red's wedding plans, the therapy center, and Matt.

I pulled into the Double R and drove down the long, dusty drive toward a classic timber-framed house. A bleached set of antlers hung above the front door. I parked in front of the three-car garage.

"Mom." The hard swallow didn't make the words any easier. "I even mentioned a prenup in case something went wrong, then I proposed to get him to stay."

"You didn't."

"I did. It didn't take him long to turn me down. He knew my heart wasn't in the right place. I was desperate."

"Desperate is never good. So—you're finding homes for the horses in an effort to free up the budget." She took off her sunglasses. "Have you considered that maybe, just maybe, Matt leaving was his way of helping you get that therapy center? He's always given you what you wanted."

"Would he really do that?" I rested my head against the headrest and groaned. "I'm a fool."

Mr. Reeves came out of the house with his dogs to greet us.

"We can finish this conversation later," Mom said.

We got out of the car. The waggling canines with sweet energy sat at my feet. My gaze met my mom's. She was right. I'd be taking them home. By Mr. Reeves's expression, he knew I'd be adopting them, too.

"Nice to meet you, Mr. Reeves. I'm Chloe McIntyre, and this is my mom, Brook." I scanned the open green pastures and impeccable fencing against a backdrop of mountains. "I can't believe you're leaving this behind. You've got quite the spread."

He tipped his hat. "Thank you. Nice to meet you, ladies. Welcome to the Double R." He wiped his brow with a bandanna from his shirt pocket. "It's never easy saying goodbye, and I've got some good people waiting for me in Oklahoma. Thought I'd be here to kick the bucket, but my family presented an offer I couldn't refuse." His brown eyes twinkled. "My wife has been gone for some time now. We had fifty-two great years here. It's time. This place isn't the same without her."

I knelt to pet the dogs.

"Sarah's been taking care of them since they were pups. They're brothers. Slim and Jax. Such good boys." Mr. Reeves patted their heads, and they laid down.

"I'll take good care of them. How would you feel about me sending you some pictures now and then?"

"I'd be mighty grateful. I hear wonderful things about the 617." He gestured for us to follow him. "I want to show you something before you leave."

We walked along a narrow path leading to the back of the house. In the clearing, three bays grazed. I leaned on the fence next to Mr. Reeves.

"I was going to take these guys with me, but I've had a change of heart. Slim and Jax would be lonely without them."

"Sounds like Sarah knew you'd take more than the dogs," Mom said.

Mr. Reeves jiggled the latch on the gate, and the horses trotted over. "Sarah was here the other day. Said they're healthy and would be perfect for someone looking for a friend."

"As much as I'd love to, I can't take your horses. You should take them with you."

"No," he said, his sigh heavy. "They belong here. If you're not interested, I understand. They've seen their fair share of years and aren't probably the kind of horses you can use working the land or cattle."

Sarah had sent me here on purpose. She knew Reeves had horses I couldn't turn down. My granddad's cattle were my legacy, but this calling to help others had consumed me when I'd met Emma. She was more than Sarah's daughter, she mirrored something in me I wanted to address, not just for her and children like her but for my daughters, too.

The crew ran like a fine-tuned machine most days. As foreman of the 617 Ranch, my role was expanding. I didn't know the ins and outs or how I'd get there, but the change was bigger than I'd ever expected. I glanced at my mom.

"Would you like to know their names?" Mr. Reeves reached into the pocket of his overalls and produced a plastic bag filled with carrot pieces.

"I don't think that's a good idea." My words were forced.

"She might not be able to walk away," Mom whispered.

"That's exactly what I'm hoping." Mr.

Reeves's black moustache twitched.

I bowed my head and put my foot on the bottom fence rail. The holes in my heart needed filling, and the only person who knew what I needed was me. "This is not what I expected."

"It never is." Mr. Reeves's toothy grin shone with wisdom. "This guy with the silver chin is Duke." He pointed to the tallest bay. "This is Mix, and this guy with the white streak on his nose is Bass."

"Very handsome." I'd woken up with an ache in my belly, and Sarah had sent me on a healing mission. The first of many to come. "If it's not too much to ask, could I have a photo of you and your wife?"

A shadow passed over Mr. Reeves's gaze.

"Thought it might be nice to have so when people stop by, my stories are complete."

"I agree. When you get home, check your calendar and give me a call. I'd like to deliver them myself."

"You got it."

"Thank you, young lady." He tipped his hat. "I thought long and hard about leaving my animals behind. Prayed the Lord would send me a shepherd." He unlatched the gate. "Come on, now. One more test before we seal the deal."

"A test?" Tests weren't my forte, hence the situation with Matt. I wiped the palm of my hands on my jeans.

He shooed the trio away. Duke glanced back with a dark stare. "He's got an eye on *every* situation around here." Mr. Reeves shut the gate behind me.

"Is there *really* a test?"

"Nope. I was wondering if you were willing to accept a challenge."

"Is she ever." Mom laughed. "I'm surprised you two haven't met before."

"My mom's right. This is my kind of challenge."

"Duke is my gauge. Animals know good people when they meet them. His bridle is on the post over there." Mr. Reeves pointed toward the watering trough.

Watching my step, I walked to the hitching post, picked up the bridle, rattled the reins, and waited. Mr. Reeves and Mom watched on.

Duke circled the pen, then eventually made his way toward me. I shook the bag of carrots Mr. Reeves had given me. We stood nose to nose, our gazes locked. "Am I worthy?" Duke sniffed the halter. "Only if you want to, big guy." He lowered his head. I fed him a couple of carrots. Bass and

Mix watched from a distance.

I walked back to the hitching post and hung up the bridle. Duke followed at a slow pace. I trusted he'd let me know when he was ready, like I should've done with Matt. I stood next to the post and waited until the bay nibbled on the bridle. I took it from the post, slid it over his ears, and stroked his hide.

"Let's do this. There's something to be said for riding bareback."

I led him to the mounting block and slipped the reins over his head. "Show me." I watched his every move. I climbed the steps and mounted him. My denim seat fit perfectly into the curve of his back. We rode around the ring, getting to know each other.

"Real nice," Mr. Reeves said. "Duke approves."

"That's my girl." Mom pushed her shoulders back and clapped.

"Thank you, sir," I said. "They say people come in and out of our lives for a reason. Some stay a long while, some a fleeting moment. The length of time doesn't influence the importance. Would you mind if I spent some time with them?"

"Take all the time you need, young lady."

"You in a hurry to get back?" I asked Mom.

She shook her head. "I'll be right here waiting."

BACK HOME, I tacked a copied list of dog commands Mr. Reeves made for me to the bulletin board in the barn office and tucked the other one in my pocket. I took Slim and Jax to the vacant pasture near the river with a bag of dog toys. Mom tagged along with a pouch of liver treats.

With a pocket full of incentives, I had Mom hold the dogs. She waited for my command to release them. "Come on, now," I yelled.

Mom dropped the long neon orange leads I'd hooked to their collars. The dogs ran past me and toward the river. "Come on, now," I yelled louder. With a sharp turn, they ran back to Mom without giving me a second look.

I followed. "Let's try it again. I'll call for them when I'm ready." They ran past me. "I did the same thing to Matt. What is wrong with me?" I whistled, and they raced to me. They sat at my feet, and I handed out treats. "Mom, call them."

"Come on, now." She waved her hands. They ran past her and scooted under the fence rail.

The grass whipped against my jeans as I chased them. Mom followed.

"I thought Mr. Reeves said they were trained," she called.

"They are, but we're not him. Come on." I jogged past her. Slim and Jax ran to the main house, parked themselves near the front door, and barked.

Maggie poked her head out. Lil sat on her hip. "What's going on out here?"

"Where's Maria?"

"She's in the kitchen. I asked her to bring the girls over. I hope that's okay." The slightest of smiles crept into the seam of her lips. "Holes."

"That aching part of you when someone leaves or passes away," I explained to my mom.

Gracie pushed past Maggie. "Dog."

Maria came to the door. "I'm guessing you took the dogs." She picked up Gracie.

"Meet Slim and Jax. Slim has the salt and pepper coat with the black mask. Jax is the color of caramel."

Slim wiggled through Maggie's legs. "Hey. Come back here." The rattle in the kitchen stopped me in my tracks. He returned with Samson's dish in his mouth and dropped it at my feet. "Hang on a second."

I filled the dish with cool water from the spigot on the side of the house near Maggie's garden and put it in the yard. The dogs lapped it up, and I refilled the dish. Tristan, Dad, Justin, and Quinn rode in. Dad stopped when he noticed the new additions.

"Thought we could use some extra help now that we're short a wrangler and his dog. Hope that's okay, Dad."

"You're the foreman. They look mighty fine. Glad to see they're not horses."

Samson appeared from behind the house. He drooled and laid on the porch without giving Slim and Jax a second thought.

Jax sat at Maggie's feet and stared at Lil. "Hey, Maggie and Coco. Can you sit in the yard with the girls?" I pulled the list of commands from my pocket, circled the girls and the grannies, then called to Slim and Jax, "Circle." I looped my finger in the air with the command and repeated it. They circled the girls, then sat at my feet. "Good boys. Treats for everybody."

Slim trotted to Mom and Maggie. Gracie laughed when he licked her hand.

"Come on, now." I pointed to my feet, and he returned. "Looks like I found myself a backup babysitter."

"You wouldn't," Mom said.

"I *would* appreciate three minutes in the bathroom alone." I tucked the commands in my pocket. "They'll be great. Now, I have to tell Dad about the horses."

"Horses," Maggie said, getting to her feet.

"Gypsy." Gracie pointed toward the barn.

"Yes, friends for Gypsy." I looked at Maggie. "I promise I'll tell him."

CHAPTER 28

MATT HAD BEEN gone five days and counting. His spotty, cryptic messages on the answering machine were hurried and clipped. Calling Branch to check up on him wasn't an option. I'd gotten what I wanted but on Matt's terms.

I didn't have to tug at the covers, wait for the bathroom, or trip over his boots in the mudroom. I spent my time getting ready for the arrival of Duke, Bass, and Mix. I'd put the first rejection behind me and found another promising donor. Sarah and I scheduled a visit to a therapy center outside Livingston. I'd made a list of questions and was eager to see their setup.

In my mind, with almost twenty-five horses gone, a therapy center was doable. Matt was still the only one I knew with grant-writing experience, but that still wasn't a reason to ask him to come home. I'd move forward alone. We were both doing what we needed to do. I'd figure out the funding on my own.

I'd promised Maggie I'd tell Dad about taking Mr. Reeves's horses, but I didn't.

Mom stayed with the girls and me. Her presence didn't fill Matt's void, but it sure did make caring for them easier. Maria loved Mom's company and crazy Hollywood fashion world stories, design, and her business partner, Hermione Crow.

Mom had spent hours creating stretchy headbands with cutouts of cowboy boots, flowers, and horses. She used Gracie and Lil as models with the intention of creating an accessory line just for them. I was sure I'd be seeing it in stores soon. Mom designed and sketched at least a dozen additional Western styles while reminding the girls that her nickname was Coco, not Grannie Brook. She and I had a conference call with Red about coming to a photo shoot at the ranch that would feature the wedding mini-collection she and Hermione had designed. Mom promised it would be low-key and that Hermione would be here to help supervise.

A quiet barn made finding those next five horses fine homes easier than expected. Sarah and Doc Neely had sent me one rancher and two families looking for animals. I'd had the opportunity to sell them all, but I turned the rancher down. I'd asked

Emma to help me feed and care for the remaining horses. I took mental notes of her behavior and observations when we worked with the them one-on-one. I reorganized my original list of horses, more than half of the fifty now scratched off, and listed the remaining horses by temperament, with Emma's help.

The office phone rang, and I answered.

"Hey, Chloe. It's Matt."

"Hi. How are you?" I peered out the window at the empty pasture.

"I'm fine. It's sure busy here. Up before sunrise and riding until dusk. Days off will be sparse for a while."

"The girls miss you. Can we set up a time to talk on the cell phone so they can see you?" I doodled on the desk calendar, counting down the minutes until Reeves would be here. "If you don't have time, I understand. Can you hold on a sec?" I held the phone away from my ear. "Don't hang up. They're coming. I can hear Gracie mooing."

Mom wheeled the wagon into the office.

"Go ahead. The girls are listening." I put the phone on speaker.

"Hey, pretty girls."

Gracie perked up. Lil played with her stuffed horse.

"Daddy's real busy. I hope you're being good for your momma."

The speaker screeched, making the girls cover their ears, and I turned it off.

"Hey, Chloe, my radio is going off like crazy. I'll call tonight around dinner. On the cell. Tell the girls I love them."

I said goodbye. My heart pinched.

"Daddy." Gracie pointed to me.

"How is he?" Mom sat on the corner of the desk.

"Busy," I said. "We really haven't had a chance to connect."

"They usually are," she replied.

I eyed the clock. "There's so much to do. Featherstone is hanging light fixtures today." I doodled a dollar sign next to his name on my list of things to do. "We're so close. Red and Bradley will be back in a couple of weeks. Hopefully, everything will be done."

"Did you tell your father about the horses?"

"Not exactly, and Reeves will be here sooner than later."

Dad appeared in the doorway without a sound.

"By the look on his face, he knows now." I frowned.

"Pop-Pop," Gracie said.

He tickled her chin. "Brook, do you think you can take the girls back to the house so Chloe and I can chat? I won't keep her long."

"Good luck." Mom wheeled the wagon out of the office.

"Thanks, I'll need it," Dad and I said in unison. Neither of us found the timing amusing.

"I'm listening." He crossed his arms over his chest.

"When I picked up the dogs, Mr. Reeves had three bays. I couldn't say no." I glanced at the clock on the wall. "His wife, Nell, depended on those horses. She loved them. He'd told me about how she took care of them. They were her reason to get out of bed in the morning when she got sick. She passed away."

"Chloe. I agreed to the barn and nothing more."

"Please—hear me out. More than half of our horses are gone. I'm making a real dent. And you've said nothing about replacing Matt." I stood and handed him my working list. "A rancher near Butte offered to buy them all, and I turned him down. Before you say anything—I left that door open. But I couldn't, Dad, at least not yet."

"I had no clue you'd find so many homes. I didn't think you'd let any of them go."

"But we renovated the barn, and I know money doesn't technically grow on trees. I wanted to follow through."

"And you thought if you made a big dent in the budget, there'd somehow be room for a therapy center." His gaze flitted around the room as he took in the black-and-white family photos hanging on the walls.

"I did the research, even got a rejection, and I'm working on the next application. If it doesn't work out, let me learn that lesson on my own. You said it yourself: you didn't think I could let the horses go, but I did. We're down to fifteen after the next five go. These three coming today—"

"Today?" Dad rubbed his stubbly chin and groaned.

"Seriously, how can you be upset? I've thinned the herd and have plans to find more of the horses homes. I won't take in any more after these three. I've listed them by temperament. They're suitable therapy animals ready to work. We can use the barn as part of the facility. We've got bathrooms, more stalls, an updated tack room, and loft for lounging or gatherings. When I told Reeves about my idea, he said his wife would approve."

"Chloe. You're killing me."

"I promised Reeves I wouldn't sell his horses. I

wouldn't have taken them if they weren't therapy worthy animals and healthy. I know this isn't what you want. It's what *I* want. Grandma and Grandpa's legacy won't go by the wayside. I promise. I love those White Park cattle as much as you do, but having the girls, meeting Emma, and realizing how important the animals are to *all* of us proves we have a bigger purpose. Mental health is important, and if we can provide positive experiences for one person by letting them ride, pet, or care for one of my horses—"

"That's not what we do here."

"Dad. What was the first thing I did when I got here?" I held his stare. "I made friends with the animals because I was lonely and sad. Mom was living far away and almost nonexistent in my world. You and I had moved multiple times. I didn't have many friends, and the ones I'd made, I left behind. You know as well as I, every barn cat, dog, horse, and cow helped me cope with childhood struggles, and they still do. So much so, I slept in the barn because I wanted Gypsy to know how important she is to me. And if her time working the cattle is done, she'll still be a working horse, just a different kind. It's time for a change. If Grandma and Grandpa were here, they'd agree."

"Chloe—"

"You said it yourself—Emma is welcome any time. What's a few more children? You were a pediatrician. Think about the kids you treated who weren't only ill but had emotional challenges or were going through difficult situations." I planted my hands on my hips, feeling the fire grow in my belly. Or maybe it was the chili dog I'd eaten last night.

"There are grants and money available to get this thing off the ground. We've got a special place here. Let's pay it forward. We could do so much."

Dad paced. "Well, undo it. If you call this guy delivering the horses today, maybe you can save him a trip." He stormed away. "There are other things to fix first."

"I *won't* undo it. Let's talk numbers." I matched his heavy strides through the barn. He mounted Breeze in a huff and galloped away.

My radio crackled. "Yeah," I said.

"There's been a delivery. It's for you," Maggie answered.

"I didn't order anything." But Maggie's voice cut out. I shook the radio, set it in the charging cradle, then hustled up to the house. Slim and Jax sat on the porch with Mom and the girls. Mom's mischievous smile rattled my nerves. "What did you do?"

"Nothing. I swear." She combed Lil's hair, then told Gracie she'd design her a fringed jacket and jeans with embroidered horses.

"Oh boy." I found Maggie sitting at the dining room table. "What's wrong? Where's Maria?"

"She's at your place doing laundry and straightening the house." Maggie slid a fancy box tied with silver ribbon across the table. "I think there's been a mix-up."

"Is this my dress for Red and Bradley's wedding?"

"Not exactly."

I removed the lid. "This *isn't* what I ordered." I fingered the tatted lace of the long Bohemian gown I'd tried on while shopping for Red, the same dress I'd found in Red's bridal magazine that gave me goose bumps. The one I'd knew I'd never wear. "Who sent this?"

"This was taped to the box." Maggie slid a card across the table. "It's addressed to you."

"Great. One more thing to fix. And by the way, Dad knows about the horses. He's mad. We also discussed an animal therapy center, which didn't go well either. He rode away. Matt called, and that was a bust. We're O for three."

Maggie listened with clasped hands. I opened the card and read it aloud.

Last year, your momma sent you a fancy pair of boots. You tucked them away because you weren't ready to accept her love. When you two made up, you wore those boots, and in time, you decided they weren't made for mucking out stalls and slugging through mud because they came from a woman who loved you.

I watched you the day you found this dress in Red's magazine. I saw you tuck the picture of it in your pocket when you thought no one was looking. Feelings don't need to be scary. The unknown can make the ride thrilling.

When I saw you in this dress, I knew you needed it. Tuck it away. Who knows, maybe someday, there'll be an occasion.

Love,
Glad

I put the card back in the envelope and laid my head on the table. Maggie stroked my hair.

"Mr. Reeves is here." Dad's voice preceded his entrance.

"I think I'll excuse myself," Maggie said under her breath. "We can talk about the dress later. Good luck."

"Thanks, I'm gonna need it," Dad and I said in

unison. Dad scowled, and we marched out of the house together.

"Thought you rode off."

"I didn't get very far. Saw the trailer pull in."

"You gonna ride off again if you don't like what you hear? I'm taking those three horses. It's a done deal. And even if we're not a united front at the moment, could you please act like it while Mr. Reeves is here? I've done everything you've asked me to. Well, almost everything. I've done the dirty jobs, trained the untamed, including the wranglers, mended fences, helped birth calves, done paperwork, made calls, gotten myself back in the saddle, and been to every meeting you've held. I've made messes and screwed up plenty, but we both know who'll be taking the reins someday, and it'd be nice if we built whatever that is together. Before you say anything, I have one question."

"Chloe, I'm not sure—"

I cut him off. "I'm not finished."

"Fine," Dad said through gritted teeth. "But I expect you in my office at seven tonight. Sharp. I'll finish my thought then."

"You didn't always agree with your father. You had ideas about how to run this ranch, too." I threw my hands in the air. "Oh wait, I'm you, just twenty years later. I want this ranch to be better than ever, and I'll do what I have to make sure it does." I turned on a heel, then swung around. "Here's the question. Did Matt take that job because of finances? Because I'm beginning to think I'm not the only reason he left."

Dad didn't answer. He didn't flinch or rub his whiskery chin like he did when he had thinking to do or buying time.

"I'll see you at seven, sharp."

CHAPTER 29

Mr. Reeves pulled in, got out, and greeted me. "The boys are here."

"This is my dad, John McIntyre."

"Nice to meet you," Mr. Reeves said. "You've got quite a daughter."

"Yes, I do." He shook Mr. Reeves's hand.

"Mr. Reeves is selling his ranch and moving to Oklahoma to be with family. He's decided his horses would be happier here. I assured him they'll have a proper home and care." My narrative was a clear message to my father. Integrity and promises were not meant to be taken lightly.

"I'm leaving the trailer. I won't be needing it," Reeves said. "I'm real happy the boys will be helping others."

Ignoring the flutter in my stomach, I squared my shoulders. "That's my intention. I don't have all the details worked out. If it's not feasible, I don't want you to be disappointed. The center is a pipe dream at this point." The words came out easier than expected. "I'm not sure I should take them since I can't promise a favorable outcome."

"I'm gonna be straight with you." Mr. Reeves shifted his stance, his expression serious. "Sarah told me there wouldn't be any better place for them than with you. My Nell lived and breathed for horses. Do you ever have days when the only thing worth living for is the noblest of creatures wearing your saddle?"

"Do I ever."

"I'm guessing our mutual friend, Emma, isn't the only one around here that talks to the animals." Mr. Reeves wiped his brow with a bandanna.

"You got that right. We've got a wrangler who sings to them, and everybody knows that I love to talk. Talking with them is different. There's no worrying about saying the right words or worrying if you've disappointed them. They're just there." I glanced at my dad. "They listen and, in my opinion, there just isn't a better companion than an animal, whether it be a horse, a dog, a cat, a cow, or a crow."

"There's your answer, Ms. McIntyre. You may not end up with a therapy center, but these three will no doubt bring you joy, and that's all I'm looking for. I don't want money. I just want to know they'll be loved like my Nell loved them."

"They will. I promise."

"When my wife and I made our way out here some fifty-two years ago, Lord rest her soul, we didn't have much. We worked our fingers to the bone, and we made something of ourselves, thanks to the help of a gentleman by the name of Cardiff. I'm paying it forward."

"I've got something to show you after we get the boys into the pasture." I radioed Maggie.

We unloaded the horses. The trio of bays meandered into the empty pasture adjacent to the corral. I secured the gate. Maggie and Mom pulled the girls in their wagon along the gravel drive.

"I'll do everything I can to pay it forward." I whistled. "Come on, now," I called. Slim and Jax came running and sat at my feet. Their tongues waggled, and their noses twitched. "Wait." I held up my hand until they settled.

I wheeled the girls to the middle of the drive and called the dogs. They sprinted, kicking up dust. "Circle," I said, looping my hand in the air. They circled the girls, then laid down next to the wagon. "Good boys."

Mr. Reeves called them over, knelt, and welcomed them with open arms. He glanced up to Dad. "Thank you for taking my animals. They'd be pretty bored where I'm going." He stood, opened the gate to the pasture, and sent them on their way. "They're a fine brood."

I picked Lil up, and Dad took Gracie from Maggie without saying a word.

"Horse." Gracie pointed to the field. "Dog. Ruff-ruff."

I straightened the headband Mom had put on Lil. She wrapped her arms around my neck. "These are my daughters; my stepmom, Maggie; and, you've already met my mom, Brook."

"My goodness." His gaze met my dad's. "You've got your hands full."

"You're not kidding," he said.

The trio came to the fence. He took a bag of carrot pieces from his pocket and fed them. "Could I stop by before I leave?"

"You can come by every day if you'd like," I said.

"Call me Beau."

"Sure thing. I'm ready to introduce Slim and Jax to the cattle. How would you feel about saddling up and joining us? Might make the transition a little easier," I said.

"I'd like that something fierce," he answered.

"How's the day after tomorrow?"

"I'll be here. You got a horse I can ride? As you know, my boys aren't working horses." Beau stroked Duke's neck. His hands had definitely worked many a year; they were thick and strong.

"We've got plenty of horses to choose from," Dad said.

I handed Lil to Mom and gestured for Beau to follow me. "Some of ours aren't working horses anymore either. They're special though. We run them every evening, then round them up in the morning. They've got easy personalities and appreciate people."

"I'm sure you'll figure it out, young lady."

"I appreciate the vote of confidence." I could feel my father's gaze upon me.

After Beau and I unhitched the horse trailer, he left.

"Seven o'clock." Dad handed me Gracie.

"Sharp. Say goodbye to Pop-Pop." The girls waved and blew kisses.

"Momma," Gracie squealed and rubbed her tired eyes.

Justin walked over, his brow pinched. "Looks like a storm is brewing, and I'm not talking about the weather."

"Do ya think?" I called Maria on the radio. When she didn't answer, I looked to Justin. "How are you with kids?"

"If your dad catches me watching those two,

he'll have both our hides, and it seems you're already skating on thin ice."

"Chicken," I said.

"I gotta go." He made his way back into the barn.

Sarah drove in and parked near the corral. Gracie and Lil's sobs faded when they spotted Emma.

"Just passed Beau. The horses must be here." Sarah tucked her keys into her pocket.

"Would you mind if Emma took the girls back to the house? I'll let Maria know she's coming." I called Maria again. "Hey there. Emma's bringing the girls your way. They're ready for a nap."

"Got it," Maria answered.

Slim and Jax sprinted in from the field.

"They're *all* here." Sarah's expression appeared nothing but pleased.

"You sent me there knowing I wouldn't leave empty-handed. I'd stay away from my dad if I were you." I forced a smile, showing all my teeth.

"I didn't know about the horses. You gotta believe me."

"I'd stick to that story if I were you."

Emma took the handle of the wagon and headed toward the house. "I can't believe how comfortable she is here. She's amazing," I said.

"She loves it here. You make it easy, and she's so excited you've taken Beau's horses. You may never get rid of us."

"I can live with that." I kicked at the ground. "You knew exactly who to call, didn't you?"

"Glad I could give you a nudge." She smiled.

"What else should I know about Beau Reeves?"

"Let's walk and talk."

LUNCH CONSISTED OF five girls around the kitchen table gabbing and gossiping. Sarah finally announced she had work to do, and Emma asked if she could stay. I gladly said yes. Maria had taken the girls upstairs for their naps. I tossed the dish towel on the counter, then sat back down at the table with Emma. Samson laid at her feet and snored. His was surely full from the scraps Gracie and Lil dropped from their high chairs.

"Why did Gracie and Lil's dad leave?" Emma asked.

"He took another job." I played with the salt and pepper shakers. Her question caught me off guard.

"I don't remember my father." She sipped her drink; the ice cubes clanked against the glass.

"Can I braid your hair?" I admired her pinstraight sleek mane as dark as the White Parks' ebony eyes.

"You would do that?"

"You've got the best hair." I took my time dividing it into three even parts. "So soft."

"Mom says I get it from my dad. He's Cheyenne."

"When you wear your hair back, I can see your cheekbones. I bet you a dollar my mom will say something about them when she meets you." I wove Emma's hair, admiring the sheen.

"I'm sorry I asked about Matt," she said. "He was super nice to me. He let me ride Trigger near the pond once when you weren't here."

I secured the tie at the end of her braid. The tassel tickled the palm of my hand. I sat, crossed my arms on the table, and put my head down.

"Does your teacher ever make your class put their heads down?" I questioned.

"Yeah."

"I liked putting my head down in school. I didn't think it was a consequence. It was a break, a time to rest and not work. That quiet time gave me time to dream about my mom or my grandpa and this ranch."

"Can I braid your hair, Chloe?" The corners of Emma's mouth lifted.

I sat up, slid the bandanna from my head, and straightened my shoulders. "I thought you'd never ask. The hair ties are on the counter." I pointed to the plastic container the girls had decorated with horse stickers. "The girls don't have enough hair for ponies yet, so my mom is designing headbands. I bet she'd make one for you, too."

Mom appeared in the mudroom doorway. "She's standing behind you. Now that she's older, she helps girls who want to be models, works with fashion designers, and designs clothes, too."

"Who are you calling older, young lady? Sixty is chic, and I can still rock a runway."

"No one. Mom, this is my friend Emma. Emma, this is my mom, Brook."

Mom inspected Emma's braid. "Very fancy. A fishbone. Chloe, you look good in a braid, too. You should wear them more often." She sat. "Moms can be lots of things. They can stay home. They can work. They can change their minds as well as the world. What do you want to be when you grow up?"

"I'm not sure." Emma stared at my mom with round, sparkling eyes.

"You know, Emma, it's been a long time since anyone has braided my hair. Whatcha think?" Mom asked.

"Your hair is perfect. I wouldn't want to mess it up." Emma lowered her lashes.

I took in Emma's hesitant expression. "She wouldn't ask if she didn't mean it."

Mom ran her fingers through her styled tresses and shook them free. "Grab the hairbrush and a hair tie."

Emma's dimples appeared. Mom told modeling stories and shared age-appropriate Hollywood gossip. Emma asked her if her friends were movie stars. When Mom told Emma her cheeks were to die for, I took a dollar from the junk drawer and put it on the table. When Emma flushed with pink hues, I took the camera from the cupboard.

"How about a photo shoot?"

"I thought you'd never ask," Mom said.

"Really?" Emma straightened her posture, her gaze sparkling brighter. "This is way better than driving around with my mom doing errands."

I took the baby monitor from the counter. "Come on, before the girls wake up." Outside, I called Maggie on the two-way radio. She needed a break. "Maggie taught me how to take photos. I'll print some for you."

"Really?" Emma asked. "Everybody's so nice here. Thank you."

And there it was, from a child's lips to my ears,

validation that the 617 Ranch was moving in the right direction.

CHAPTER 30

AFTER DINNER, I hand-washed the dirty dishes and Mom dried. "What a day," I said, watching the water spiral down the drain.

"Why don't you use the dishwasher?" Mom folded the damp towel and set it on the counter.

"Washing dishes was something Matt and I did together. It gave us time to talk, unwind, and settle into evening without the day's leftovers."

"You will recover," she said.

"I know. Having Emma around this afternoon was good. Her father left, never came back. Wanted to be a rodeo king. Sarah said he didn't want a family."

"It happens, Chloe. We both know this."

"Yes, we do." I stared at her. The hair from her braid was frayed. Her muddy boots sat next to the door. She didn't seem to mind the imperfections, and I was grateful. "Maybe I'm like Emma's father."

Mom sat at the table and wrung her hands. "Hardly. You kept the children. If we're being honest, *I'd* be the rodeo king. You're overthinking your situation."

Guilt slithered into the conversation like a preying rattler.

"Hardly. You came back. And who knows, maybe Emma's dad will, too." I changed the subject. "Maggie's got another coffee table book in the works."

"She showed me the photos. She's very talented." Mom smiled. "You're lucky to have her, but you already know that."

I rubbed my belly. "Man, that barbeque pork didn't settle." Mom felt my forehead with the back of her hand. I got up, burped, then found the antacids in the cupboard. The fruity, chalky tablets coated my mouth.

"Stress will do that to a girl. By the way, I need to be home by Tuesday. You were great with Emma today. I meant what I said earlier. Moms can do anything they want. What's right for you may not be what's right for me, your dad, Maggie, Matt, or any of those other hunky wranglers." She touched my heart with her fingertips. "You're the only person who can determine the journey."

"When did you get so spiritual?"

"I love my life coach. I've learned a lot about myself. And Hermione's been a wonderful role model."

The rise of emotion caught me off guard. "I'm so proud of you." I wrapped my arms around her and squeezed until she squealed and wiggled free.

"I wouldn't be here if it weren't for you."

"You've done everything all by yourself. You're so independent. Always on a mission." I held my mother's aquamarine gaze.

"I could say the same about you. I've also learned that working with a partner makes the load lighter and a whole hell of a lot more fun if you respect each other." She smoothed down the front of her blouse. "You're always on my mind. Pushing me forward. Challenging me to break down isolating barriers."

"I challenge a lot of folks around here. Hope they *all* don't leave."

"Never." Mom pushed in the dining chairs. "I'll check on the girls."

The mudroom door clapped shut. The methodical footsteps were familiar. I waited for Dad to show himself.

"It's not seven yet." I leaned against the counter. "Mom can watch the girls."

"I know." He scratched his whiskery chin. "There's something I'd like you to see."

I slipped into Matt's denim jacket I'd taken from his duffel and put on a beanie. Mom had her feet up on the ottoman, leafing through a fashion magazine. Lil and Gracie played with toys on the floor.

"Dad's here. I'll be back."

"I'll get them ready for bed."

"Thanks." I turned on a heel, then glanced over my shoulder. "Mom—"

"Yes." She looked up from the glossy pages filled with elegant Western designs.

"Thanks for the talk."

She shooed me away. Outside, the lights in the renovated barn radiated from the skylights. The warm glow made everything about this day better.

"Chloe."

"Yeah, Dad."

"When I agreed to renovate the barn, I did it because I couldn't say no. I want this place to be everything your grandparents imagined it could be. Budgets are always an issue. I'm overly protective when it comes to providing for your future and the girls."

"I know. I've seen the books. Money comes and goes, and waiting for the next influx can be taxing." I tucked my hands in my pockets. "You never answered my question earlier. Did Matt take that job because of our finances?" When my father said nothing, I balled up my fists.

"Not exactly," he answered.

"What do you mean, *not exactly*? Tell me."

"Tristan, Silas, Quinn, Justin, Matt, and I were talking."

"Sounds like a meeting I wasn't invited to."

"It wasn't a meeting—just some cowboys talking on a lazy ride toward a smoldering horizon. Listening to their dreams took me back to a time I rode alongside my parents. I wanted to renovate the barn as much as you did." The hazy evening light intensified my father's dark stare. "Matt and I talked numbers later. Numbers turned into a cowboy heart-to-heart I hadn't expected. When you were adamant about not getting married and the bickering began, he put in his resignation. The boy wanted to marry you. He loves you, like Winston loved my momma.

"Branch's offer came with a nice salary and an opportunity to buy more cattle at more than a fair price. I said I'd keep Matt's Angus until he's ready to move or sell them. I really thought I'd be attending your wedding before Bradley and Red's. I couldn't say no to the barn reno because I thought this was the place you and Matt should be married. I wanted you to find love."

"I thought I had. Everything was going so well, until it didn't." The evening chill crept into my veins. Stupid pride. "Did you know your momma bought cattle before your parents had this place? They had nowhere to put them and—"

Dad touched his fingers to my lips.

"If you think about it, he's helped free up the budget in his own way. He's given you everything you've wanted. He told me you mentioned a prenup."

I lowered my gaze. "I did. I don't like messes."

"Life is messy."

We walked into the old barn. It smelled of fresh stain, sawdust, and possibility. The dusty veil removed. I ran my hand along the wall, imagining my grandparents' setbacks and togetherness. I opened the stall doors, inspecting the finished areas. I made my way to the stairs leading to the loft. Red and Bradley's wedding would be the only wedding the McIntyres would throw here, and I'd accepted that reality.

"We should go upstairs," Dad said.

Wrought iron fixtures cradled bare bulbs over-head. Mr. Featherstone and Mr. Cortright had fashioned a rustic bar with four saddled stools. The sepia tones begged for company. Two leather sofas and two heavy cowhide chairs were arranged around a rustic coffee table at the opposite end of the loft, below the window. The faux bear rug had been altered and draped over the back of one of the sofas. "I didn't order the sofas, chairs, or coffee table. By the way, the bear rug looks nice without the menacing stare. Kudos to the person who lopped it off. We didn't discuss a bar either."

"I know. That was me. The furniture, the rug. The studded coffee table was Maggie. She bought it the day you went dress shopping in Bozeman."

"Send it all back if we need the cash."

"This place is special. You've got all these ideas of how to make things better. I'm set in my ways."

"What else did you do I don't know about?" I walked to the middle of the room. My footsteps echoed in the open space.

"I consulted the financial planner. We discussed selling acreage."

"Selling land is crazy talk. Why would you do that?"

"That's what the financial planner said. Everything is paid off. Keeping tight purse strings means you and the girls will have everything you need, and you'd be able to have your therapy center."

"Not that way, Dad. Ever. Everything I need is standing right in front of me. Well, almost everything."

I'D GOTTEN UP early, gone to the barn, and saddled the horses before the crew straggled in for the morning run. Gypsy and I stood together at the fence, discussing life as the sun pushed away last evening's blanket. I knew in my gut what needed to be done.

After the horses had been corralled and the wranglers had begun the day's work, Mom met me at the hitching post where Big Red and Buttercup waited. Dad joined us.

"I know that look." Mom raised her manicured brow, her blonde curls knotted at her nape.

"Everything's a mess, mostly me. The barn is beautiful, there's a dress in a box that I can't stop thinking about, and Matt's too damn far away."

"The Chloe I know would do something about it. Do you love him?" Mom asked.

"I'm scared." I held her stare.

"The Chloe I know is fearless, loves with her heart. There isn't anything more powerful than that." Mom wrapped her arms around me. "There are no guarantees in life. Changing your mind doesn't make you weak. It makes you human. And it doesn't mean you'll end up divorced like your dad and me. I don't regret marrying your dad—I regret how it ended. We didn't love each other like you and Matt do. Don't let our marriage define your future. That boy would follow you to the end of the earth. You two are grounded like Winston and Ida May.”

“That’s what Dad said.” My gaze met his.

“Don’t live your life based on our misfortune. What are you waiting for?” Mom added.

“Your mother’s right. What are you waiting for? Seems to me you know what you want.”

“Chloe, we all lose our way. You’re hell-bent on learning your own lessons, but for once, can you lead with your heart, not your head? What’s it telling you to do?” Mom clasped her hands at her heart.

“I never regretted marrying your mom. Something beautiful came from that relationship. I just wish we hadn’t fought the entire time. You deserved better from us. Not getting married may ensure a divorce-free life, but you’re missing so much. When you say *I do*, it makes you work so much harder for that relationship. You can’t live happily ever after fearing an ending that may never come.”

“And when it’s all said and done, you don’t want to regret giving up something you were meant to have all along,” Mom added.

I HUSTLED BACK to the house, told Maria I was leaving, packed a bag and a satchel of snacks and a small cooler. There was a lot of thinking to do between here and Branch's Wyoming ranch. I wasn't sure the five-hour drive would be enough time to buy into my impulses or not long enough to convince me to turn around and come home.

Branch's ranch was marked with a black wrought tree above the curly wrought iron gateway. The road to the main house seemed a mile long and led to acres and acres of flat land. The mountainous backdrop was detailed with harsh rock and snowy peaks.

Trigger was tied to the hitching post near a red barn closest to the red gabled house. I parked the truck, honked the horn hoping to get someone's attention, then got out and stretched my legs.

A dusty wrangler appeared from a shed.

"Hi, there. I'm looking for Matt Cooper."

The wrangler frowned, pointed to the red barn, and disappeared back into the shed.

"Well. He wasn't very friendly." I hadn't questioned my motive to be here until now. The open doorway to my left was marked with a sign that read Office. It was empty. The tap on my shoulder startled me, and Matt caught me by the elbow. Lola planted her paws on my thighs and barked.

"You scared me to death."

"What are you doing here, Chloe?"

"I came to see you."

"A phone call would've been better. Did you bring the girls?"

Matt's grumpy tone sucked the excitement from my very core.

"No girls. Would it have made a difference if I had?"

"It's been a long day. I wish I would've known you were coming. That's all."

Matt showed me into the office.

"If I would've called, you might've told me not to come."

"Must be pretty important."

"Remember when I asked you to marry me? Of course you do." I breathed in an invisible balloon of courage.

"Chloe—"

Matt pulled out a red vinyl chair from the table, and I sat. He sat across from me. My heart pinched. I couldn't believe he'd chosen this place.

"Please, Matt. Let me finish. Please come home. I love you." My hands trembled.

"Behind the scenes, I pushed for the barn reno because I thought you'd say yes to marrying me, especially after Red and Bradley accepted the invite to get married there. Thought you'd get the bug to tie the knot, too. You went shopping, organized details, even agreed to a photo shoot with your mom at the ranch. Which I thought totally went against everything you stood for when it came to publicizing our private life. Not to mention, I had accepted the co-CEO position. Seems like you wanted everything except what I had to offer. I wanted you to be my wife."

"Did you want that more than wanting me to have the therapy center?" My heart answered before Matt could. "Is there any chance?" The words drifted between us. His clouded gaze took my breath away.

"This is where I belong. I've accepted that, and coming to Wyoming was the break I needed. I lost myself doing things your way, and when you threw in the idea of drawing up a prenup, I understood more than ever that you need to stand on your own two feet and so do I."

"Are you sure this is what you want?"

"It's what I need right now."

"Well, this didn't turn out the way I thought it would. I'm sorry I hurt you." I stood, turned on a heel, and left the office.

"Chloe—"

I didn't acknowledge his call. Heat rose to my

cheeks as the impulse to flee consumed me. I couldn't change Matt's mind any more than I could control the situation, and I ran out of the barn.

"Looks like you found Cooper." The dusty cowboy I met on the way in leaned against the fender of my truck. "I'm available though."

"I'm not and never will be." I got into the truck, revved the engine, then drove away.

CHAPTER 31

W HEN 4:00 A.M. rolled around, the hazy weight of the day stirred, and getting up after a sleepless night seemed reasonable. I showered, dressed, ate toast, and told Mom I was heading to the barn. I left her with the radio and wrote Maria a note.

My warm breaths turned to white puffs of ice crystals as I tried to warm my hands.

I turned on the light in the barn, made my way into the office, turned on the coffee machine and the space heater. The sound of Tristan's gait greeted me before he did.

"I forgot you're an even earlier riser." I poured him a cup of coffee.

"You look terrible," he said.

"And good morning to you, too." Then I poured myself a cup of coffee and sipped it. It wasn't nearly as tasty as Matt's brew. "You don't look much better."

"Maggie will have a spread after we round up the horses. The herd's getting mighty thin." He set his empty coffee cup on the table.

"My first proposal got shot down. Even with the visitation Sarah and I have planned, the dream seems further away than ever."

"Does it?" Tristan poured himself more coffee.

"He gave me the world, and I blew it."

"Love makes people do strange things."

"I'm a fool. Let's get those horses saddled. It's gonna be a long day."

"Chloe, he may not work for Branch forever."

"Forever," I muttered under my breath. "That's a funny word. Well, since the offer was so great, there's a good chance he will. Cattle, money, a place to live. Doesn't get much better than that."

"I beg to differ." Tristan stared into his coffee. "Vivian and James were my forever. I followed Viv on a whim and ended up here. Strange how the world changes our plans."

The bitter coffee soured my stomach, and I put it down. "We should get to work."

AFTER RUNNING THE horses, I slipped away to the renovated barn. I sat alone in one of the new stalls on a bale of hay. Coal curled up in my lap. She purred while I bared my soul.

"I blew it. I cut him off and convinced myself I

wasn't marriage material before he even had a chance to propose." I stroked her back. "The house isn't the same without him. His side of the bed is cold. I've got no one to heckle. I knew I loved him, but I didn't know how much. And I'm sitting here wearing his jacket I stole from his duffel. I'm a thief. It smells like him, and I love that. At least I'll have that."

I sat up with a start as heavy footsteps neared. Coal leaped from my lap and scampered away. I didn't move. I didn't ask who was there. I wanted to be invisible. I covered my face, and when I looked up, Matt was staring down at me.

"What are you doing here?"

"I needed my favorite jacket. Could've sworn I packed it." He showed me the jean jacket I'd swapped for his. "This isn't mine. Pretty sure it belongs to you."

"Guess you packed in a hurry."

"We both know that's not true." He raked his fingers through his hair. "Got room on that bale of hay for a tired cowboy?"

I unbuttoned the denim jacket I wore, inhaling his scent, wanting to take it with me wherever I went for the rest of my life.

"We'll trade in a minute. I think we both know I'm not here for that jacket. Yesterday didn't go so

well, and there is something I want to ask you."
He sat and took my hand. "After you left, I
brawled with the mouthy wrangler you met."

"Are you serious?"

"Yes. Branch and I had a long talk afterward."
Matt pushed his bangs back and showed me a cut
along his hairline. His shoulders fell forward with
a hard sigh.

"I quit. After you drove away, I knew I'd made
a mistake. If a prenup is really that important, I'm
sure we can work something out." He wrapped his
fingers around mine.

When I started to speak, Matt touched his finger to my lips.

"The thing is, you *are* my world, and so are the
girls." He opened a velvet box he'd pulled from his
pocket. Inside was a Montana sapphire solitaire set
in platinum with gold accents. "I know they're
your favorite."

"Only second to you." I held his dark gaze.
"There'll be no prenup. I'm so sorry I screwed this
up. I laid awake last night praying you'd come
home."

Matt took the ring from the box and slipped it
onto my finger. I wrapped my arms around his
neck, then kissed him.

"You're gonna need a wedding band." Matt

took a silk pouch from his other pocket. "Bradley and Maggie wanted you to have Glad's ring."

I read the inscription: Love always wins.

"Yes. It does. I'll wear it every day just like she did." As much as I wanted to slip it on my finger, I placed it back into the pouch for safekeeping. "You really quit?"

"I knew if I worked myself into Branch's world, I'd regret it. I also knew that if I didn't ask you to marry me, I'd regret that, too. And we promised each other, no regrets."

"I love you, Matt Cooper. Don't ever leave me again."

"I love you, too, Momma."

His mouth covered mine, and I kissed him like I'd never kissed him before. Lola ran in, barked, and wedged her way between us. There was a knock on the stall door.

"Excuse me," Mom said. "There are two little ladies out here wanting to know if their momma said yes."

"I did." I showed her the sapphire ring, then Matt slipped it on my finger. It was a perfect fit.

Lil and Gracie toddled in. Matt and I scooped them up and shared the good news. Lil handed me a daisy, and I stuck it behind my ear.

"Your dad would like to see you two," Mom said.

"Should we show your momma what I brought her?" Matt kissed Gracie's cheek, then tickled her.

Gracie tugged at my sleeve. "Horse. Horse."

Matt led me outside. Tied to the hitching post was a beautiful chocolate speckled Appaloosa.

"You brought a horse with you? Should you tell my dad, or should I?"

"He knows. Meet Stitch. He's my wingman."

"And they just keep coming. And that's mighty all right by me."

MATT AND I sat across from Dad.

"Welcome back, son. Coming back has a price though. We're looking for a co-CEO with grant-writing experience. Are you up to the task?"

Matt nodded and shook Dad's hand.

"Does this mean you've changed your mind about a therapy center?" There was a hitch in my breath.

"Let's give it a shot and go from there," he replied.

I popped up from my chair. Dad motioned for me to sit back down, so I did. He held the rusty horseshoe I'd dug out of the mountainside the day Gypsy and I fell.

"We've got some other serious business to discuss. Did you spit on this thing before you brought it home?"

Confused, I shook my head.

"I figured so. Guess that would explain all the turmoil and unexplained hard feelings."

"What are you talking about?" I leaned against his desk.

"Legend has it that if you find a horseshoe, you should spit on it, then hang it over your door. Let's go." He pointed to the hammer and nails.

Dad stood, put on his hat, and marched out of his office, horseshoe in hand. Matt and I followed.

"Since this is the door you use most"—Dad pointed to the back door of our house—"the shoe should go here." He handed it to me. "Go ahead, spit on it."

I looked at Matt.

"Do as he says. He's gotten you this far."

I'd never considered any horseshoe bad luck, but I wasn't going to question the legend my father spoke of. My gaze met my dad's. The breeze raised the hairs on the back of my neck, and I spit like I'd never spit before. Dad hoisted me up, and I nailed the horseshoe above the door he'd run in and out of a million times growing up. Matt had me pound in three extra nails to make sure it was secure before Dad put me down.

"I forgot to mention. Beau Reeves really admires your spunk and wants to help with the therapy center." Dad shook Matt's hand, then pulled him in for a backslapping hug. "We're gonna have ourselves a wedding. Hot damn."

CHAPTER 32

TWO MONTHS HAD come and gone. Autumn was in full swing. Glorious colors trickled into the valleys with cooler temperatures.

I stood alone, admiring the flowing dress Glad had sent me in the full-length mirror. Mom, Maggie, Red, and the girls would join me soon.

I opened Matt's letter and read it. Our decisions had been met with validity and confirmed there was only one place we belonged. The 617 Ranch was our home and always would be. In the spring, we'd open a therapy center for children. We'd kept ten horses and would use the renovated barn as a safe haven for those who needed it. Gypsy's prognosis for making a full recovery was unknown, and I accepted the possibility she might never be the wild thing she once was, but being together meant we were living our best lives. She'd always be my best girl, and now it was time to share her with others.

The knock at the door drew me from my thoughts. Lil and Gracie ran into the room wearing crowns of daisies and flower girls' dresses Red had picked out. Maggie, Mom, and Red followed.

Mom handed me a bouquet of wildflowers, gladiolas, sage, the last two yellow buds from Granddad's bush on the ridge, and thistle. Mom straightened the thin straps of my dress.

Maggie stood behind me, gazing over my shoulder into the mirror.

"Sometimes a vision is a mere reflection of what *we* need," she said.

"And, if that someone is savvy enough to work, dreams come true." I smoothed out the front of my dress. I blew Gracie and Lil kisses, and Maggie took photographs.

"You're a beautiful bride, Chloe," Mom said, touching my cheek.

"Thanks, Mom." I glanced at Maggie, then to Red, and then to my girls. "I can't stop smiling."

Maria poked her head around the corner. "Is it okay if I come in?"

"Of course it is. Get over here." I hugged her. "You're one of us now. The girls would be disappointed if you didn't sit with them."

Lil touched the tatted insets of my dress with her sweet little fingers. Her dark eyes took in the intricate stitches.

Red nodded. "When I saw this gown in the

boutique that day, I knew you had to try it on, and Glad knew you had to have it."

"Speaking of presents." Mom opened her clutch and produced a baby blue box tied with white ribbon.

I opened it. Inside was a silver heart necklace just like the one I'd lost in the river. "It's perfect." I undid the clasp and put it on.

Then Mom handed Maggie a gift, insisting she open it. Gold foil paper fell away from a framed photo of Red and me. We posed with two of Grandpa's White Park heifers, their white hides and black features as elegant as the wedding gowns we wore that Mom and Hermione had designed. Maggie dabbed the corner of her eyes with a tissue.

"I knew you had to have this. It'll be part of the magazine's exclusive spring wedding issue, but it won't be released until after their wedding. Bradley won't have a clue what dress Red chose unless someone tells," Mom said.

We all locked our lips and threw away the invisible keys.

"I can't believe I get to be married in one of your gowns and that I'm going to be in a magazine modeling your dresses." Red beamed.

"And I can't believe I let my mother talk me into being part of the shoot. Best day ever."

"Just like old times. You'll always be my Paris girl, Chloe."

"Paris girl." Gracie blew Coco a smooch.

"Hey, look what I'm wearing." I lifted my skirt and showed off the studded cowboy boots Mom had sent me when I was pregnant with the girls. I'd saved them for a special occasion, and today was the day.

Gracie pointed. "Boots. Every color," she said.

"Good girl." Mom knelt before her. "That's right, every color."

"Coco, I love you." Gracie kissed Mom's cheek and touched her shiny red lips.

"I love you, too, sweetheart."

Sarah and Emma came into the room with baskets of rose petals. "We're looking for the flower girls."

Gracie clapped and Lil twirled.

"I can't believe this is happening," I said to the group of women who completed my circle.

"How about a few more poses before we get this shindig started?" Sarah took Maggie's camera and snapped photos.

"You ready?" Maggie asked.

"Ready," Lil said.

Emma took Gracie's hand, and Sarah took Lil's.

"Let's get your momma married," Sarah said.

Gracie blew me a kiss, and we walked to the barn. The hazy evening hours were upon us. The misty afternoon shower had drifted away and brought clear skies. The loft glowed with warm light. When the breeze kissed my neck, I knew Grandpa Winston, Ida May, and Glad walked alongside me. When I'd said I'd make this place into something so special no one would ever want to leave, I meant it.

Sarah and Emma helped Lil and Gracie upstairs. Mom and Maggie followed. I fingered the miniature horseshoe sewn to the ribbon on my bouquet. Dad waited for me on the landing.

"Hi. You're beautiful. Inside and out." He gave me his elbow. "You ready?"

I nodded, then kissed his cheek. Mom, Maggie, and the others made their way to their seats. Lil and Grace ambled down the aisle, tossing rose petals into the air. They giggled and emptied their baskets at Matt's feet.

"I love you, sweetheart." Dad pulled me close.

"I love you, too."

Sarah dimmed the overhead lighting. Twinkle lights sparkled, candles glowed, and Matt, handsome as ever in his western tux, waited at the other end of the loft in front of the picture window. My breath caught in my chest.

Dad and I strolled down the aisle. He stood by my side until it was time to give me away. I held his hand like I'd done so many times before. He kissed my cheek, then Matt and I said our vows.

When the service was over, Bradley played "Harvest Moon" through the sound system, and Matt and I danced our first dance as husband and wife.

"I'll always have your back, Chloe McIntyre."

"And, I'll have yours, Matt Cooper." I glanced down at the little girl tugging on my dress. I picked Gracie up, and Matt scooped Lil into his arms, and we swayed together until the song ended. After champagne was served to the intimate crowd, our guests made a circle around us.

Bradley raised his glass. "To love and happiness."

"To stubborn wills and true hearts." Dad tapped his chest.

"Let faith guide you." Maggie blew two kisses.

"And dreams inspire the obstacles." Mom curtseyed.

"May your days be many." Tristan tipped his hat.

"Make room for laughter and forgiveness." Justin stepped forward and kissed my cheek. "Leave time for quiet conversation where no words are needed." He clinked his champagne flute to Matt's.

"Dance to a happy tune," Silas sang.

"Your paths are now one journey." Red and Bradley shared a kiss.

"Hold hands and trust each other's guidance." Sarah held Tristan's hand.

"Embrace whatever comes your way with the strength between you." Maria set her glass down, knelt, and opened her arms to Lil and Gracie. They wiggled free from us and went to her.

"When separated, love long-distance." Matt's mother kissed his cheek.

"Let your spouse be your copilot. Let pride enjoy the scenery." Matt's dad hugged him. "I'm proud of you, Matthew."

"Listen to the words in the wind from those who came before you. They're always close." Trout clicked his tongue and winked at Hermione, the woman who completed him.

"To love," Mr. Reeves added.

"To us," Matt and I said in unison.

A boisterous round of cheers filled the rafters. Mr. Reeves shook Dad's hand. Emma beamed as she watched her mother and Tristan exchange glances.

Dad stepped forward. "When we began our Montana journey, it was you and me, kid. We came here to help my father, Winston, run the 617 Ranch, and along the way, we formed the family we both yearned for."

"I call them strays who know a good thing when they see it," Trout joked.

Everyone laughed.

"When the circle grows so do our hearts, and we become stronger. Look around, Chloe and Matt. This is your family, and we're here to support you when you're flying high and feeling low. We love you." Dad's dimples emerged. He raised his glass. "To Chloe and Matt."

"To Chloe and Matt." Everyone clinked their crystal glasses and sipped champagne.

"I think we have some celebrating to do," Bradley announced.

"Amen," Trout said.

Matt kissed me and downed his champagne. I stared into my bubbly, knowing I carried an unexpected wedding gift.

"You're not drinking your champagne." Matt's eyes grew wide.

"No, I'm not." My smile grew, and I glanced at my belly. "No twins this time, Cooper. Just a healthy baby boy."

FOLLOW ME:
Linda's Website & Newsletter:
www.lindabradleyauthor.com
Linda's Amazon Author Page: amzn.to/3rzhA1G
Facebook: LBradleyAuthor
BookBub: bookbub.com/profile/linda-bradley
Instagram: lindabradleyauthor
Twitter: @LBradleyAuthor
Goodreads:
goodreads.com/author/show/6498473.Linda_Bradley

Reviews and recommendations are much appreciated and can be submitted on Amazon, BookBub, or Goodreads.

NOTE TO READERS

Dear Reader,

Thank you for reading *Showdown*. The characters of the 617 Ranch hold a special place in my heart, as do readers like you!

Should you select one of my books for your book club and would like to invite me to a meeting, email me at LBradley@LindaBradleyAuthor.com. Please write BOOK CLUB in the subject line. Let me know a bit about your group, how many members you have, where you meet, and which book you've read. We can meet via cyberspace or in person, should you live local to me. If I don't respond, please reach out on social media. Glitches sometimes happen.

Feel free to send me a photo. I love seeing my books being read in a favorite place.

Thanks again for picking up a copy of *Showdown*!

Sincerely,
Linda Bradley

Linda's Books

Unbranded
(Montana Bred Series Book 1)

Threatened by the unexpected, devoted rancher—Chloe McIntyre refuses to compromise her ambition or her legacy.

Reunion
(Montana Bred Series Book 2)

Chloe McIntyre must find new ground with her mother, especially since she is now going to be a mother herself.

Showdown
(Montana Bred Series Book 3)

When emotions clash, Chloe McIntyre and her beau, Matt Cooper, redefine their happily ever after.

Maggie's Way
(Montana Bound Series Book 1)

Middle-aged Maggie Abernathy just wants to recuperate from cancer, but when Chloe and John McIntyre move in next door, somehow her empty house becomes home again.

Maggie's Fork in the Road
(Montana Bound Series Book 2)

Just when Maggie Abernathy thinks she's got her life in order, she faces loss and makes an unexpected friendship.

Maggie's Montana
(Montana Bound Series Book 3)

Maggie Abernathy makes good on a promise that changes her life forever.

A Montana Bound Christmas: Ho, Ho, Home for the Holidays!
(Montana Bound Series Book 4)

Unexpected guests and a lost dog bring the *Montana Bound Series* cast of misfits together for a special Montana Christmas.

The Montana Bound Series on Amazon:
amzn.to/3rzhA1G
The Montana Bred Series on Amazon:
amzn.to/2WtkQJk

More by Linda

Pedal

Can a whisper from beyond give middle-aged Paula Murphy, burdened by heartache, the courage to just pedal?

Coming back to her Bay View summer home in northern Michigan means more than planning picnics at the beach and working in her daughter-in-law's bicycle shop. Her avoidance to embrace her grown son's death isn't the only tribulation weighing on this self-reliant social worker's mind.

Reluctant to believe the unfathomable, Paula Murphy's world is turned upside down when she's reunited with the only man she's ever loved.

Pedal on Amazon: amzn.to/3rzhA1G

About the Author

Linda's inspiration comes from her favorite authors and life itself. Her character-driven stories integrate humor found in everyday situations, family drama, and forever love. Her distinct voice creates memorable journeys and emotion.

Linda's been a finalist in the Booksellers Best Contest and Romance Reviews Readers' Choice Awards. She lives in Michigan with her artist husband, sons, and rescue dog. Linda loves art, animals, and stories with hope and heart.

9 780999 579398